MY OWN PERSONAL ROCKSTAR

KIRSTY MCMANUS

www.bloodhoundbooks.com

Print ISBN: 978-1-5040-8551-9

CHAPTER 1

TASH

*O*kay. I'll admit it. I'm lame.

You're not supposed to have a crush on a reality TV singing contestant. That's reserved for thirteen-year-old girls and people who have no lives – not busy thirty-five-year-old single mothers.

"Tash! It's back on!"

I hurry to the lounge, balancing four bowls of Ben and Jerry's on a tray. I unceremoniously dump three of them into outstretched hands and sit down next to my bestie, Millicent (or Missy, as she prefers to be called) and start shovelling that heavenly ice cream into my mouth. Mmm... eye candy and literal candy. (I got the flavour with those little chocolate-covered caramel chunks.)

"You almost missed your favourite contestant," Millicent teases.

"Come on. I can't be the only one who loves Lincoln Page."

Millicent looks down at the floor, where my six-year-old daughter Daisy is sitting cross-legged, eyes glued to the screen. She's so entranced by what she's watching, she attempts to spoon some ice cream into her mouth and misses. It lands with a plop beside her.

Millicent laughs. "I'm guessing your daughter is also a fan."

Normally I would pick up any spilled food immediately, but for now, I'm leaving it. Lincoln Page is about to perform on *Sing to Me*.

"I wouldn't say your son is any better," I point out as her little boy rubs his food-covered hands in his hair.

"Yeah, but that's Ryder. He's not hypnotised by the curly-haired rock god on the screen."

"Shh, he's starting," I hiss.

Millicent rolls her eyes but stops talking so we can fully appreciate the spectacle that is Australia's *Sing to Me* semi-final. There are only six contestants left, and Lincoln is one of them.

The audience cheers as the lights go down. The studio band plays the opening chords of INXS's 'Never Tear Us Apart', and a single spotlight illuminates Lincoln in all his beautiful glory.

Tonight, he's wearing black leather pants and a loose black T-shirt. His ebony curls are perfectly defined, falling to just above his shoulders.

But it's not even the fact that he's insanely hot I find the most attractive. It's that he seems like a genuinely nice guy. Throughout the whole series, he has been super supportive of all the other contestants, and he looks as if he's really enjoying the journey, constantly smiling and bantering with all the mentors and backstage crew.

When he starts, the audience almost overwhelms his voice with their appreciative cheers. That slightly raspy tone channelling Michael Hutchence causes my skin to break out in goosebumps.

"He's good, isn't he, Mummy?" Daisy says.

"He's very good."

Lincoln grips the microphone with both hands and soulfully sings about two people meeting by chance and not wanting the connection to end. He closes his eyes, making me feel as if he means every single word. On the final note, he reopens them, and the intensity with which he looks down the camera and directly into my soul makes me shiver.

Everyone in the audience jumps to their feet, clapping and whooping.

"I suppose that was okay," Millicent concedes.

"*Okay?* We *were* watching the same thing, weren't we?"

"All right. He was impressive."

"Will you vote for him?"

"Will I be welcome back in this house if I don't?"

"Not for at least a month."

She mock sighs. "Okay. I suppose I can spare my *incredibly* valuable consumer power for you."

I log onto the show's website with my phone and cast my vote. "Who else would you pick?"

"Honestly, if it were up to me, I wouldn't choose anyone. I'm not a hormone-driven teenager."

"But it's fun, lusting after a rockstar on TV. Where else can you obsessively watch a hot guy and not get into trouble?"

She smirks. "You, my dear, are a lost cause."

I pick up her phone from the coffee table and shove it at her so she can process her vote. "You see the appeal though, right?"

"Sure. I mean, I don't love long hair on a guy, but Lincoln Page definitely has the 'it' factor."

"Can I vote, Mummy?" Daisy asks.

"Sorry, baby, you have to be over sixteen. But you can share mine."

"I hope he wins!"

"We'll find out soon enough."

Lincoln is the last singer of the night, and the voting lines close after a recap of the evening's performances and an ad break. I really hope he does well. My slight infatuation with the guy spans longer than just this season of *Sing to Me*.

Fourteen years ago, when he was twenty-one, Lincoln won a different talent show called *Have You Got What It Takes?* Back then, he was cast as a Robbie Williams clone, his curly hair cut short and straightened. Every week, he sang a bunch of bland pop songs that he performed perfectly in a technical sense (hence the reason he won) but I got the impression it wasn't the style he preferred. He released an album that did amazingly in the charts, but his follow-up didn't have the same success, and he soon faded into obscurity.

I moved on, and actually kind of forgot about him until he showed up as a contestant on this season of *Sing to Me*. Now my crush is back in full force, and I'm glad he's expanded into music a little more to my taste.

The host appears on the screen, along with all six of the finalists. Lincoln is standing at the end, beaming his trademark smile.

"Sadly, we have to say goodbye to three of these amazing voices tonight," the host informs us. As if we don't already understand how a reality singing show works.

She opens an envelope.

"The first person not going through to the final is… Kennedy Young."

A petite country singer with long red hair looks suitably crushed, but she manages not to cry as she accepts her fate. She's standing next to Lincoln, and he gives her a consolation hug. I sigh.

Millicent looks at me. "Are you *jealous* of Kennedy?"

"No. Maybe," I admit.

"You do know Lincoln has a partner and twin girls, don't you?"

"Yes. Yes, I do. But I can still dream."

"As long as you don't start writing him fan mail asking him to leave his family for you."

"I wouldn't do that! But just so we're clear, I'm allowed to like his Instagram posts, aren't I?"

She shakes her head. "Would me saying no actually stop you?"

I don't bother dignifying her comment with a response. But mostly because the host is talking again.

"The second person leaving us tonight is… Tyler Finlay."

A twenty-something rapper grimaces and nods. Lincoln gives him a complicated high-five that doesn't look even remotely rehearsed. He's so cool.

"And the third person to not make it through…"

I hold my breath.

"…is Lincoln Page. I'm so sorry, Lincoln. You've definitely been a fan favourite this season, and I hope we haven't seen the last of you."

The crowd roars a combination of support and shock. I stare at the screen. Poor Lincoln.

But his smile doesn't waver as he takes the microphone to acknowledge those involved with the show. "Thanks, guys. I've had the best time this season, and I'm so appreciative of everyone who helped me get this far. Also, I want to say a massive thank you to Rachel and my beautiful little girls, Isabella and Madison, for being so supportive while I pursued my dream. This was all for you."

The camera pans between Lincoln and his family in the front row as he blows them a kiss.

"Aw, your boy is gone," Millicent says. I can't tell if she's secretly happy or not. She didn't watch him during his first stint on reality TV so she clearly doesn't have the attachment I do.

"I want Oliver to win," Ryder declares.

Oliver is a Michael Bublé wannabe. I feel he would have done well ten years ago, but his sound would be hard to brand in today's market.

"Sure, we can root for Oliver," I say, trying not to show how much Lincoln's elimination has bummed me out.

"Can they still give Lincoln a recording deal?" Daisy asks.

I wrap my arm around her shoulder. "I hope so. I guess we'll have to wait and see."

Millicent stands. "We should probably put you two munchkins to bed. Daisy, your mum has a big day tomorrow."

The kids complain, but I echo Millicent's statement. "That's right. I have to leave early, so I need a good night's rest."

Tomorrow, I'm flying to Sydney to pitch to the acquisitions department of a chain of independent supermarkets to try to convince them they should stock my bento boxes. My business is a meal delivery service that creates cute and healthy lunches for schoolkids. My mum's Japanese, so I've been to Japan a lot, and a few years ago I became obsessed with the art of designing edible masterpieces with a few simple ingredients.

My favourite thing to do is create animals and cartoon characters out of rice, egg and seaweed. I started uploading photos to Instagram, and almost immediately, people asked me where they could learn how to make them, so I ran a few online tutorials. But it turned out everyone really just wanted the finished product, so I began working with a chef to have them made in bulk to sell at markets.

From that point, it snowballed. I now have a website where customers can order my stuff directly, and after tomorrow, I'm hoping to start stocking them in the refrigerated section of supermarkets throughout the east coast.

I get the kids organised with their toothbrushes and give Millicent a quick hug. "Thank you so much for looking after Daisy while I'm away."

"It's cool. Your place is nicer than mine, so I'm happy to stay here. Plus I expect a very expensive present once you land this deal."

"No problem. What are we talking? A fancy dinner at Urbane? A sports car?"

"Yeah, I'm thinking along the lines of a new Audi convertible," she says, eyes twinkling.

I laugh. "We'll discuss this again if I get the contract."

"You're totally scoring that contract. Now go on, get your beauty sleep. I'll see you when you're back."

I kiss Ryder on the top of his head and pull Daisy in for a big noisy kiss on the cheek. She shrieks. "Mum! You put spit all over me!"

I playfully wipe her face with my hand. "Love you, honey. I'll probably be gone before you wake, but you know you can get Missy to call me if you want anything."

"I know. Love you too."

I tuck her into bed and make sure Ryder's comfortable on the floor on the trundle before checking that Millicent's set for linen in the spare room.

I head to bed and lie there, staring at the ceiling. My brain is a jumble of thoughts.

As I drift off to sleep, flashes of bento boxes and Lincoln Page blend together in a nonsensical montage of weirdness.

I hope one day I can find my own rockstar.

CHAPTER 2

LINCOLN

I walk backstage and let out a deep breath. So. It's over. I'm not quite sure how I feel yet. On the one hand, I'm disappointed, because of course I wanted to win. But on the other, it's kind of a relief. After what happened the last time I won a reality singing show, I was scared of history repeating itself.

The rest of the cast and crew are waiting for me in the wings, and they all line up to give me the obligatory post-elimination hug. I knew it was coming because I'd done the same thing to all the other contestants who left before me.

"Well done, mate," my mentor, JC, says as he pats me on the back. "You did me proud."

"Thanks. Sorry our team didn't win."

He waves a hand dismissively. "It's just a show. It doesn't mean anything in the scheme of things. What's important is what you do next. You've built up a decent fan base, so you need to capitalise on that now. What's the current situation with your band?"

I've been in a cover band for the last ten years. We mostly play local gigs, but the pay is barely enough to support my family.

When it's particularly slow, I work as a barista at a friend's coffee shop in the city.

"They're eager to get back to a regular playing schedule. Obviously, I haven't been around much, so they've suffered a bit financially."

"Well, I might be able to do something about that. I was talking to-"

"Lincoln."

I turn to see Rachel and the girls standing behind me. The twins run up and each grab one of my legs.

"We'll finish this conversation later," JC says. "Come find me when you're done."

"Will do." I bend down and wrap the girls in a hug. "You two are up way past your bedtime."

"But we're not tired, Dad!" Isabella protests.

"Yeah, we're big girls," Madison adds.

"I never said you weren't. But it's getting late. I have to stay for a bit longer, otherwise I'd come home with you right now. Mummy will take care of you tonight, and then I'm all yours from tomorrow onwards."

"So that's it?" Rachel says. "You're done?"

"I guess. I mean, I'll be in the finale for a couple of group performances, but that won't require much time to rehearse." I look up at my beautiful partner and see she doesn't seem particularly happy. "Are you all right?"

"I'm just disappointed."

I stand so we're at the same level. "Because I didn't win?"

"Of course! You worked so hard for this. I thought for sure you'd make it to the end."

"It doesn't matter. It was a great experience, and I managed to get my name out there again. I'm sure that can only mean good news for the band."

She doesn't say anything. I didn't realise she was so invested in the outcome.

I kiss her on the forehead. "Don't be sad. This is all good. Hey, do you want me to see if we can get a babysitter for the girls, and then you can hang out with me tonight? We'll have a few drinks…"

"No, no. I think it would be best if I took the girls home myself. They've had enough excitement for one day."

"As long as you're sure. I won't stay out all night – probably just an hour or so to thank JC and the crew. Is that all right?"

She nods. "Come on, girls, we need to go."

"No! We want to stay with Daddy!" Madison wails.

Rachel looks at me for support. "A little help, please?"

I crouch back down and give Madison a kiss on the cheek. "Princess, this is grown-ups time. You'll be bored if you stay, but I promise I'll make it up to you tomorrow. Maybe we can go to South Bank and get ice cream from Messina?"

She pauses as if contemplating the offer. After an unspoken conversation with her sister, she gives me a thumbs-up. "Okay."

I kiss Isabella on the cheek too. "I'll see you both in the morning." I shoot Rachel an appreciative smile. "Thanks, babe. I owe you."

"You do." She grabs each girl by the hand and leads them away.

I try not to take Rachel's reaction personally. I just need to give her time to come to terms with me not winning. It's strange, but I don't feel as bad about the outcome as she clearly does. I really do believe that the band will get a boost from this experience – and that's all I can ask for. If I'd won, there's no telling what the label might have demanded. They could have insisted I go solo… or change the style of music I perform…

"Link!"

I blink. Grayson, one of my fellow contestants, is trying to get my attention.

"We're all heading to Cloudland for something to eat and drink. You coming?"

"Is JC going?"

"Yep."

"Okay. Cool." I figure I can briefly celebrate my time on the show and still get home for a decent night's sleep.

Because even though this whole adventure has been exciting and intoxicating, there's still nothing better than curling up next to Rachel and having the girls climb into bed with us first thing in the morning.

Family is everything.

THE SHOW HAS RESERVED a decadent VIP booth at Cloudland filled with velvet cushions and red chiffon curtains. There are about fifteen of us: a mixture of the final contestants, some of the mentors, and a few behind-the-scenes crew.

I sit beside JC and sip a glass of red wine someone handed me. JC drinks bourbon straight. I've never seen him order anything else, although I've really only hung out with him for rehearsals and a couple of these events. I don't go to every elimination party because I'd rather be at home with the girls.

"How are you feeling?" he asks.

"Good. I'm going to miss all of this though."

"Yeah, it's hard to go back to normality after such a high. But it's important to put it all in perspective. I think you've got your head screwed on straight, and you're keeping it real with your family. I was too stupid at your age to realise how important being grounded is."

JC is an old-school rocker from the eighties. He toured the world with his band for the better part of three decades until they finally called it quits.

"You did okay though," I point out.

He snorts. "Professionally, yeah. Personally, I was, and still am, a mess."

"It's never too late to settle down," I tease. "I'm sure you'd still have the ladies lining up around the block for you."

"That's the problem. They are. But not for boring old John-Carrol. They want JC Tarik."

I laugh. "John-Carrol? Is that what your initials stand for?"

"Yes. Popular to contrary belief, I'm not Jesus Christ."

"Why doesn't anyone know this?"

"Because I only tell my friends. And they understand the consequences should it somehow be leaked to the media. I legally changed my name to JC when I first signed with Intergalactic Records back in 1982, so for all intents and purposes, John-Carrol is dead."

"Duly noted. So does this mean you consider me a friend?"

"You know I do. And you'll want to propose marriage after I've told you my next bit of news."

"Oh?"

"Earlier, I talked to Max, and he wants to meet with you to discuss a national tour."

My eyes widen. Max is JC's manager. "What?"

"It's all hush-hush at the moment, so you can't even tell your bandmates until after the meeting, but he's been really impressed with your performances and the feedback I've given him. I told him he'd better get in quick before someone else does."

A dopey grin forms on my face. "You did that for me?"

"Like I said, the show wasn't important. What happens next is."

"Thank you so much! You've already been more than generous with your time and advice. I don't know how I can ever repay you."

"By not screwing it up. And by being you."

"Aw, thanks, dude. I won't let you down."

JC holds up his bourbon. "To world domination."

I clink my wine against his glass. "To world domination."

JC slams back the rest of his drink, and I finish my wine. Then I have a thought. "Does this potential tour include my band?"

"Of course. I know you're loyal to those guys, which is why I said they'll hopefully forgive your absence up until now. A national tour should keep you going financially for the rest of the year."

"And Max is okay with this?"

"Yeah, I showed him a clip of one of your gigs, and he was sold. He likes that you already have a solid dynamic with the guys."

"That's great! I guess I should find out when he's available to meet."

JC removes an envelope from a pocket inside his jacket. "Here's your plane ticket. You're flying to Sydney first thing tomorrow morning."

I laugh in surprise. "Seriously?"

"I thought I'd make it easy for you."

"This is too much. You can't buy me a plane ticket and set me up with your manager!"

"I just did. Also, there's a room at the Shangri-La waiting for you afterwards."

"Oh my God."

He claps his hands together. "I think we need more drinks. Make the most of this night."

"Can I share the news with Rachel?"

"Maybe just tell her you have to go to Sydney as part of a contractual obligation for the show, and then you can surprise her afterwards."

"Okay, cool."

I get out my phone to text her. I pause, remembering I promised to hang out with the girls tomorrow. Hopefully they'll understand. I'll just have to postpone our outing until I get back. If we have enough money to live comfortably for the rest of the year, I'm sure Rachel and the twins will be supportive. Rachel's family lives in the UK, so we might even be able to afford airfares to go visit.

> Hey, baby. I have to fly to Sydney tomorrow for a thing to do with the show. My flight leaves early, so please apologise to the girls for me and tell them I'll make it up to them. And I promise I'll make it up to you too. I love you!

She doesn't reply, which is understandable if she's putting the girls to bed or has already gone to sleep herself.

While I would still love to be with them, you don't get opportunities like this every day.

And I'm going to make the most of it.

CHAPTER 3

TASH

*T*he next morning, thanks to a traffic jam on the way to the airport, I almost miss my flight. I race through check-in, glad I only have a carry-on, and bolt to the boarding gate.

"Just made it," I say breathlessly to the flight attendant checking passes. "I got stuck in traffic."

She smiles politely, but I can tell she's heard that excuse a million times. I'm normally quite organised and allow extra time in case of such a hold-up, but this morning, Daisy woke early and decided to have a clingy moment. When she begged me not to go, I was *this* close to booking three extra tickets and dragging Millicent and the kids along to Sydney, but Millicent managed to distract Daisy with pancakes long enough for me to sneak out.

If I didn't have Millicent, I don't know what I'd do. My parents help out a lot, but I can't rely on them all the time. Mum is a teacher at a primary school (sadly not Daisy's) and Dad is always travelling for his work as a software sales manager (he met my mum when he was in Japan on a business trip) so their schedules aren't very flexible.

It's times like these when I wonder what it would be like if

Daisy's father, Brad, was around. Not that I actually want that man anywhere near us. He made his stance very clear when he found out I was pregnant after we'd been dating for a year. *I'm not ready to settle down, cliché, cliché, cliché.* He didn't even stick around long enough to find out if I was having a boy or a girl. And when I tried calling him after Daisy was born, I discovered his phone had been disconnected. As a result, he didn't get a mention on the birth certificate.

I make my way down the tunnel connecting the terminal to the plane and smile guiltily at the next attendant waiting patiently to direct the last of the passengers to their seats.

"Just to your right and down the back," he says.

"Thank you!"

I avoid eye contact with my fellow travellers, who are already seated with their carry-on luggage stowed. Of course I'm in the back row, maximising my exposure to everyone on the plane.

I spot the only empty seat left, which is thankfully on the aisle, and plonk down.

It takes a second to register who's sitting next to me.

Oh. My. God.

My heart starts racing. Am I hallucinating? Maybe I'm still sleeping and just thought I woke up and got on the plane. After all, this man did occupy a significant portion of my dreams last night.

Lincoln Page.

I sneak a glance at him. He's reading the in-flight magazine, and I'm pretty sure he's on his own. I quickly scan the surrounding rows for signs of his partner and kids, but they're nowhere in sight.

I think I'm about to hyperventilate.

I belatedly realise my carry-on won't fit under the seat in front of me, so I have to get back up and find a space in the crowded overhead compartment. I'm so jittery, my bag slips from my hands.

Lincoln looks up. "Are you okay? Do you need some help?"

Agh! Lincoln Page is talking to me!

"Uh, I think I'm all right." I make a second attempt and feel my shirt ride up. My bare belly is practically in his face, but I can't do anything about it until I secure my bag. I slam the overhead compartment door a little too loudly and yank my shirt down. I sit back in my seat and fasten the belt. "Sorry about that."

"What are you sorry for?" he asks, smiling.

I don't think my mouth is capable of connecting with my brain.

"Oh, just for being disorganised and making a spectacle of myself. You're Lincoln Page, right?"

"I am." He holds out a hand for me to shake. "And you are?"

"Tash. Natasha. Northwood." I don't know why I added my last name, but it sort of popped out accidentally.

"It's nice to meet you, Tash Natasha Northwood."

I giggle. "Tash on its own is fine." I hold on to his hand a fraction too long and suddenly rip it away when I realise it might seem creepy.

He pretends not to notice and gestures at my head. "Hey, I like your hair."

"Thank you. It cost a fortune to have done but I think it's fun."

Eek, am I rambling? I'm totally rambling.

"Is it supposed to look like fire?"

"Yes!" I turn so he can see the back. "I used to have it only orange, but then I saw a picture where someone had the same colour and then added pink and red streaks to make it look like flames, and I knew I had to copy it."

"It's very cool."

"*Your* hair is very cool," I say, wishing I could reach out and touch it.

"Thanks. It's a bit of a mess today, but I didn't really have time to do it properly. I was at an after-party for the show last night, and I found it difficult to sleep when I got home."

I stare at his tangled curls, and I can't help wondering if that's how he'd look after a session in the bedroom.

It takes a second for me to formulate an intelligent question. "Are you disappointed you weren't in the final three?"

"Do I look disappointed?" His trademark grin is ever present.

"No?" I guess.

"Exactly. I'm not, because I'm off to Sydney this morning for a secret meeting."

"That sounds intriguing."

"I'm not really allowed to talk about it yet. But hopefully soon."

The plane taxis for take-off but I barely notice.

"Please let me know if I'm being too personal, but how did you end up back on another reality show?"

"Well, it wasn't something I would have sought out on my own, but the producers at *Sing to Me* wanted to mix it up a little this year, so they invited a whole bunch of people who had already experienced some level of success in the past. That's why you probably recognised a few of the contestants."

He's right. At least six of the first-round singers had been one-hit wonders or child stars at some point in time.

"I just assumed they changed the rules this year, allowing a wider variety of people to try out."

"Technically, that's true, but I wouldn't have applied unless they asked me. Anyway, enough about me. What do you do?"

It takes me a moment to remember because I'm hypnotised by his liquid brown eyes.

"I… uh… I run a food delivery business for schoolkids' lunches."

"That's awesome. I know Rachel and I are always struggling to think up new ideas for the girls to take to pre-school."

I get out my phone and open the photo gallery, relieved my limbs are obeying me and not freezing up in superfan-induced fear. "This is the kind of stuff I do."

I hand him the screen, and he flicks through the images. "Holy shit. You made these?"

"I did."

"Even this one?" He points to a photo of a box containing nine rice balls that look like kittens.

"Yes. Admittedly that dish took a while to do."

"My girls would love these!"

"If they're anything like my daughter, Daisy, they'd probably like this one." I scroll to a lunchbox with a teddy bear theme.

"How do I get these?" he demands.

"I... I have a website."

He picks up his boarding pass and a pen. "Write it down for me. I'm going to show the girls when I get home."

I shyly oblige, wishing I could ask him to write something on *my* boarding pass. And then I have a brainwave.

"Would you mind signing an autograph for Daisy? She's a huge fan."

He chuckles. "Of course."

I hand him the card and watch as he scrawls a message.

> Dear Daisy,
> Thanks for listening to my music! It's amazing to know I have fans like you.
> Have a beautiful life.
> Lincoln.
> P.S. Your mum is very talented!

I read it and smile. "Thank you so much! She's going to love this."

"No problem."

The food cart comes by and interrupts our chat. I figure I should give Lincoln some space, so I eat the breakfast wrap the attendant hands me while reading through the notes for my meeting on my phone. But I can't concentrate. Having this rock god sitting inches away from me is making me giddy. His arm accidentally brushes mine and I feel like I've been zapped.

"Oh, sorry, did I hurt you?" he asks when I jolt.

"No! I'm just nervous. About a meeting I have today." Phew. Nice save, Tash.

"What's your meeting for?"

I explain to him about my appointment with the supermarket people, and he nods, impressed. "Going by what I've seen, you definitely deserve success. So it looks like we both have interesting things happening today."

"If your secret meeting doesn't turn out the way you want, I'll be very surprised," I say.

"I appreciate your vote of confidence."

The rest of the flight goes way too fast. I think I could stare at Lincoln forever and not get tired.

When we land, since we're right at the back, we're the last to disembark, but it still doesn't feel like enough time. At least I didn't get a chance to freak out too much about my appointment.

We're about to go our separate ways in the terminal, and Lincoln waves. "Good luck today. You're going to kill it!"

"Thank you! You too! I'll keep an eye out on social media for what's happening with your music."

I watch him walk off, almost fanning myself. Millicent will find it hilarious when I tell her what just happened.

I take a deep breath. All right. Fun time is over.

Now I'm ready for business.

SOME OF LINCOLN'S stardust must have rubbed off on me because my meeting goes even better than I expected, with the acquisitions department practically agreeing to stock my meals before I've even opened my mouth. Of course, they have a whole bunch of stipulations, and they want to maximise their profits, but I come out of it with a deal I feel is more than fair. Our lawyers are going to talk next week and make it all official.

I whip out my phone the second I'm sufficiently far enough away from the supermarket headquarters and call Millicent.

She answers immediately. "How did it go?"

"So, so well! They love the product, and they're going to start stocking it in July."

"Well done, babe! I'm really happy for you! And now for me too! I've been looking at the Audi website today, and I've picked out this cute little silver number..."

"Ha-ha. Oh! I have other news! You wouldn't believe who I was sitting next to on the flight here!"

"Who?"

"Lincoln freakin' Page!"

She cackles loudly. "Seriously? Did he need to have you restrained by the flight crew?"

"No! I'll have you know I was cool, calm and collected the entire time, thank you very much. I did not try to maul him, as much as I would have liked to. I respect that he has a partner and family."

"Good for you. Was he just like he seemed on TV?"

"Oh God, yes. Missy, he was so nice! And he even asked about my business!"

"Aw, that's sweet. I guess I'll have to prepare myself for endless talk about Lincoln Page once you get home, huh?"

"If I were to die today, I'd be a happy woman."

"Well, don't go accidentally wandering into traffic. You have an empire to expand and a daughter at home who needs you."

"Duh, of course. I was being silly. Anyway, I should probably go check into my hotel. I'll call again later when Daisy's home from school."

"Okay, bye!"

I book an Uber and have it take me to my accommodation at

Cockle Bay Wharf. After checking in, I open the minibar and celebrate my new business deal with a bunch of tiny spirits mixed with Coke. I don't even mind that I'm on my own. Daisy's my favourite person in the entire world, but having a day off from the school routine and all the work that goes with being a single mother is heaven.

I switch on the hotel's cable TV and locate the music channel. It's blaring a setlist of nineties pop. Perfect. I dance around the room, singing along.

When I get tired of that, I open Instagram on my phone and navigate to Lincoln's account. I don't actually follow him, because it would be kind of embarrassing to make my reality TV crush public – especially since I only have the one account for my business. I have a lot of followers, thanks to my bright photos of fun food. Pining after a reality singing star does not quite fit the image I'm trying to portray.

I'm very tempted to start following Lincoln now, but I chicken out at the last minute. If he checks his notifications, he'll make the connection immediately, and it'll be mortifying to have him know I'm still thinking about him hours later.

His newest photo was only posted a little while ago: a picture of him standing outside a big building with one hand doing the rock 'n' roll sign. On anyone else, it would look like they were trying too hard, but Lincoln pulls it off. Probably because you can tell he's enjoying himself and not taking the situation seriously.

I read the caption.

Exciting things are afoot!

There are dozens of comments already, with people telling Lincoln he was robbed and should have won the show. I read through every single one. He has a lot of fans.

I pause on a comment that looks like it's from a friend of his called Felix.

Are you in Sydney, man? You want to meet up tonight at Nicky's Bar? 9?

There's actually a reply!

Sounds great. I'll call to confirm.

Oh my God. Did Lincoln Page just tell everyone where he's going to be tonight? Does he not realise how many people follow him? That place is going to be insane.

I google the venue. It's only two blocks away.

No. I'm *not* going to stalk Lincoln at a bar. I look at the time. It's seven thirty.

To distract myself, I scroll through his other Instagram photos. There's one of him with his partner and girls. I look at how happy they all seem together, and my heart breaks a little. I wish I had that. Not with Lincoln – although, of course in another universe that would be the dream – but someone who gazes at me the way he gazes at Rachel and the twins.

It'll happen for me eventually. I'm sure of it.

CHAPTER 4

LINCOLN

J'm almost more nervous than I've been at any of the previous elimination shows on *Sing to Me*. Maybe because this is real life now and not a game.

I head inside a nondescript building on King Street in Sydney's city centre. Apparently this is where Max Hargreaves, manager extraordinaire, works from.

There's no one at reception, so I follow the instructions on the text JC sent me and take the elevator to the tenth floor.

On arrival, I see there's no one at this reception desk either, but I can hear music coming from down the hall. I follow the noise, identifying the song as 'Macarena'. I hope it's not indicative of Max's taste. But then he's represented JC through a long and successful career so I shouldn't judge.

I reach the office at the end and pause in the doorway. An older guy with a shiny bald head is facing away, looking out the window and moving his head from side to side in time with the music. Wait. Is he also doing the arm movements?

I clear my throat, and he spins round.

"Lincoln! You made it! Sit down, sit down." He points to a chair I'm slightly disconcerted to see looks like a baseball glove.

I perch awkwardly inside the mitt and smile at Max. "Thanks for taking the time to see me."

"Nonsense. I've been watching you all season and hearing the good things JC's been saying about you. I know you've been through all this bullshit before, so I'll get straight to the point. You have potential, and I want to make money from that. I'm thinking a national tour with at least thirty dates."

"Seriously?" My brain feels like it's about to explode already.

"Yeah, I saw the voting data from the show, and you have a *lot* of fans. Your social media tracks well too. Do you know your most popular demographic is women in their thirties and forties?"

I feel my face get hot. "Uh..."

He laughs. "They see you as approachable. You're their age, and they remember you from the old days. It's hard to make a tour work for many of these reality stars, because all-ages gigs don't sell well, and it's often kids who watch shows like *Sing to Me*. But the data showed you appealed to a wide cross-section of viewers. It's not just the cougars, but women in their twenties, and pretty much all guys over eighteen are fans too."

I'm not sure I agree with him using the term *cougar* for any woman over the age of thirty but I get what he's saying. And I suppose it's all quite flattering. Obviously, not appealing to teenagers is a little bit of an ego-bruising but I can live with that.

"That's really great. It sounds very positive."

"It is. So if we do this tour, can you and your guys be available at a moment's notice?"

"Of course. I mean, JC told me to wait until I'd seen you before telling the rest of the band the news but I'm sure they'll be as excited and ready for this as I am."

"Good, good. I'll have my assistant talk to your assistant, blah, blah, blah."

I don't want to tell him I don't have an assistant, so instead I say, "Thank you, sir. I won't let you down."

"Just call me Max. None of that 'sir' crap."

I smile. "Sorry. Max."

"Okay. Now get out of here. I have a waxing appointment in five minutes, and the woman's coming here to the office."

I blink. Right. I'm too afraid to ask what he's having waxed. "No problem. Thanks again. I'll… uh… see myself out."

I stand and leave the office, dazed. Did that really just happen? Could it be that easy?

I get out my phone and call Rachel. She doesn't answer so I leave a message for her to call me back. Out on the street, I head in the direction of my hotel, not really paying attention to my surroundings. I don't come to Sydney very often so I should be making the most of it but I'm too distracted. I'm going on a national tour!

I can't wait to tell the guys. And thank JC! I lean against a nearby wall and shoot off a few texts. I see I have a ton of notifications on Instagram, so I scroll through a few. Most of them are fans, and their loyalty makes me smile. I'm so glad I'll be able to play for them again.

And then I see a message from Felix. I was going to call him while I was down here if I had the chance, but he contacted me first. And via a public comment on Instagram, of all things.

Are you in Sydney, man? You want to meet up tonight at Nicky's Bar? 9?

I should probably reply privately, but the possibility of being ambushed by a bunch of people at this late notice on a Monday night is small.

Sounds great. I'll call to confirm.

I make my way back to where I'm staying at the Shangri-La. My room has an amazing view of the historical Rocks area, with the Harbour Bridge in the background to my left and the Opera House to my right. It doesn't get much more iconic than that.

I stare out at the scene, intermittently being interrupted by phone beeps from the guys replying to my text. They sound as excited as me.

My phone finally rings with Rachel responding to my voice message.

"Hey!" I say, knowing I sound like a little kid hopped up on too much sugar.

"Hey. How's your work thing?"

"Actually, I didn't want to ruin the surprise until I knew for sure but I just came from a meeting with Max Hargreaves. He manages JC's career."

"Oh?"

"Yeah, he's organising a national tour for me and the guys! Isn't that amazing?"

She takes too long to reply. "That's great," she says eventually.

"What's wrong? Are you worried I'm not going to be around as much? Because I'll make sure I'm close to home whenever possible. And the three of you might be able to come along to some of the shows. Maybe Sydney and Melbourne?"

"Maybe," she says neutrally.

"Rach! Why aren't you happy about this? I thought it's what you wanted. For me to be successful with my music career."

"I guess I don't want to get my hopes up. Have you signed any paperwork? How many shows is it? How come they're not offering you a recording deal or any international dates?"

I laugh. "Honey, you're getting way ahead of yourself. I literally just came out of the meeting. But Max said they're thinking about thirty shows! And a national tour is only the starting point. Of course, if it goes well, they'll consider recording deals and international venues. We have to take it one step at a time."

"But you've already paid your dues. Surely ten years of local gigs is enough to prove you're worthy of more."

"Please don't worry about any of that. Enjoy the fact that it's all finally coming together!"

"I guess…"

I hear a noise in the background. "Is that the girls? Can I say a quick hello?"

"Uh, I might have to call you back later. I think Madison's trying to cut Isabella's hair."

"Oh. Definitely sort that out. Call me tonight! I love you."

"Love you too," she says, sounding distracted. She hangs up, and I look back out at the harbour. Rachel's reaction wasn't exactly what I expected, but I'm too happy to let it bother me now. She's probably just overwhelmed from looking after the girls while I'm away. Twins can be exhausting.

My phone rings again almost immediately. It's Felix.

"Oh, hey, buddy. I was just going to call you."

"How's my favourite rockstar?" he teases.

"Good. Great! I just met with JC's manager, and he's organising a national tour for me and the guys!"

"That's fantastic! Well done."

"Thanks!"

"Where are you staying? I'll come meet you, and we can have a celebratory drink before heading to Nicky's."

"I'm at the Shangri-La."

"Wow. You really are moving up in the world. Okay, I'll text you when I'm on my way."

"Looking forward to it."

I head for the bathroom to take a shower, a huge smile on my face.

This is it. I'm on my way.

§♠

AFTER BATHING, I change into some fresh black jeans and a grey T-shirt. I dry off my hair and rub some product through it. It's hard to make curly hair look good all the time. I wish I had the *Sing to Me* stylists on hand every day. Not that I enjoy being waited on, but on the days I don't wash my hair it looks messy and fuzzy so I usually tie it up.

I watch a bit of the in-house cable before heading downstairs to wait for Felix. After ordering some red wine, I sit near the window and contemplate how far I've come.

I had a fairly modest upbringing. I'm an only child but I'm not close to my parents. They've always been heavy drinkers but in the last few years they seem to have taken a turn for the worse. I'm not even sure they remember they have a son most of the time. They live down near the New South Wales border, just over an hour in the car from my place. The last time I tried to see them, Dad was out at a pub but Mum didn't know which one. And Mum could barely string two sentences together. I tried for years to get them into AA to no avail.

Eventually, I had to give up – especially once I had children of my own. I couldn't be dedicating large chunks of time to saving two people who didn't want to be saved.

I now only call them on their birthdays, and I can't imagine they'd care if I told them about my tour news. I'd be surprised if they even knew I was on *Sing to Me*.

I met Rachel just out of high school, so she's always known about Mum and Dad. She used to get frustrated with them on my behalf, constantly seeing how they were ruining their lives and ignoring their son. And while Rachel and I have been a bit on-again-off-again over the years, our relationship is a million times healthier than the one my parents have. I think because Rachel and I met so young, we needed a bit of space every now and then to grow as individuals before reuniting.

But now with the twins, we've made the commitment to stay together permanently. We've talked about getting married, but Rachel wants to wait until the girls are a bit older and can be left with friends or family while we go on our honeymoon.

"Lincoln!"

I look up and see Felix standing over me. I get up and

embrace him. Felix is a good friend but because he lives in Sydney I don't get to see him very often in person.

"Hey! It's been too long."

"I know. Let me just get a drink, and you can tell me all about how you're conquering the world."

I smile and watch as he talks to the bartender. Felix is a very attractive man. Tall, lean, square jaw, and perfect dirty blond hair. He's also gay, much to the dismay of many women I've seen approach him over the years.

Today, he's wearing distressed denim jeans and a dark blazer over a stripy T-shirt. I always feel inferior next to Felix. Not only does he have great taste in clothes, but he's also a smart and confident guy. I have to work extra hard when I'm with him.

He returns from the bar and sits opposite me, sipping something clear from an old-fashioned glass. "So tell me what's been happening with you since the last time we spoke. I need to know everything."

I grin. Felix always knows how to make someone feel special. His company is exactly what I need tonight. And while it feels slightly disloyal to have the thought, I'm kind of glad I'm down here in Sydney so I don't have to deal with Rachel's disappointment.

Right now, it's all about the celebration.

CHAPTER 5

TASH

*B*ecause I was up at 5am, and I have another early-ish flight tomorrow, I decide I should go to bed soon. But I'm too wound up, and I pace restlessly around my room.

I video call Millicent at 8pm so I can see Daisy and say goodnight. I wave at her tiny face on the screen.

"Hey, sweetie. How are you?"

"Good. How was your meeting?"

"It went well. Thank you for asking! And do you know who I saw today?"

"Who?"

"Lincoln Page! I got him to write you a message!"

She squeals. "Really?"

"Yes!" I hold up the boarding pass so she can see. "I'll give it to you tomorrow."

"He's really handsome, isn't he, Mum?"

"That he is." I sigh.

Millicent sticks her head in the frame. "Stop pining after someone you're never going to see again."

"Actually, I know for a fact he's going to be at a club two blocks away in an hour."

"Is he doing a show?"

"Oh, no. At least, I don't think so. He's meeting up with a friend."

She narrows her eyes. "How do you know that? Did you steal his phone?"

"Of course not! He posted it on Instagram."

"That was silly of him."

"I know."

"Are you going to go?"

"You should go, Mum!" Daisy says, excited.

"No, I'm not going," I say firmly. "It would be weird."

"Oh, go on. Do it for Daisy," Millicent teases. "Get a photo of him for her to go along with the autograph."

"Hang on. Didn't you just say I should stop pining for him?"

"I don't even know what I'm saying anymore," she says. "Ryder had a bad dream last night and insisted on sharing my bed, so I barely got any sleep. That kid is like an octopus on caffeine."

I laugh. "You poor things."

She tilts her head to the side. "You know, if you did go see Lincoln, you could ask him to post a picture of one of your bento boxes on his account. He has a lot of fans, doesn't he?"

"About thirty thousand."

"And he asked about your business."

"No. I couldn't do that. That would be even weirder than just going to the bar to stare at him."

"I don't know. It could mean extra profits. And you'd be able to buy me that Audi for real."

"I'll think about it," I say, shutting down the conversation. There's no way I'm asking Lincoln Page to endorse my brand.

"Okay, well, we'll see you tomorrow. Sweet dreams!"

"You too. Goodnight, Daisy. And say goodnight to Ryder for me."

"I will."

I hang up, shaking my head. Millicent's crazy.

꿿

ALL RIGHT. Maybe I'm the crazy one.

After going to bed and failing miserably to fall asleep, I jump back up and put on a pair of loose-fit jeans with a black halter-neck top. I slide into some white tennis shoes and head out the door, grabbing my purse on the way.

It's amazing how if you really want to do something – even if you know it's dumb – you can find any number of ways to justify your actions.

And I've managed to come up with three perfectly good reasons why I should be going to Nicky's Bar:

1. I didn't eat a proper dinner, so I'm actually quite hungry, and I don't want to pay the extortionate prices they charge for room service at the hotel.

2. I may have misunderstood Lincoln's Instagram post, and he could be performing tonight after all. It makes sense because you'd have to be pretty clueless to tell thirty thousand fans you were heading out for a quiet drink with a friend. It could be a marketing ploy, and he's really doing one of those 'secret' gigs like the one Prince did in London that time.

3. Okay, I don't really have a third, but I'm going to borrow Millicent's suggestion and pretend that I might actually ask him to endorse my brand. I would never really do that, but two reasons didn't seem quite enough.

Despite my justification, I know this is a bad idea. I should've at least worn a hat. My flame-coloured hair stands out a mile away. The only consolation is that the club should be so busy, there's no way Lincoln will spot me.

But when I reach the entrance, there are fewer people than I expected. I suppose it *is* a Monday night, and Lincoln only posted the message a few hours ago. Plus, not all his fans would be over the age of eighteen and living in Sydney. But still.

I contemplate turning around and going back, but I figure I've come this far. I might as well have one drink – and maybe a bite to eat.

The place isn't particularly big, but there are at least fifty people scattered about inside. Enough for me to not be immediately recognisable.

With my back against the wall, I do a quick scan of the nearby faces. No Lincoln.

Unsure whether to be relieved or disappointed, I go to the bar and order a mojito, taking it over to a white leather couch in the corner where I won't look so obvious. It's been forever since I've visited a place like this. Single mothers don't get a lot of free time.

At least the music is fun – a continuation of the nineties pop that was playing in my hotel room. I bob my head along to 'Everybody' by the Backstreet Boys and sip my cocktail while reading the food menu. I start to relax, and I'm glad I came out. I deserve to celebrate after my success today.

And then my stomach does that swoopy rollercoaster thing as I notice Lincoln and another guy walk over to the bar. I assume he's with his friend Felix. Did they just arrive? I hope they haven't already seen me.

God, what am I doing? I was worried about what he'd think if I followed him on Instagram, but having him spot me here would be a million times more embarrassing!

I figure I'll finish my drink and discreetly leave when they're no longer standing in the path to the exit, and he'll never even know I was here.

They collect a couple of beers and start making their way over to my part of the club. I prepare to be sprung and brace myself for the impending mortification.

But it never comes. They veer off to the other side of a nearby partition and disappear from view.

Phew. I'm safe… for the moment. But from their current position, they'll still see me if I try to leave. I'll have to stay put for a bit longer.

I attempt to make myself as inconspicuous as possible, pressing against the couch and tying my hair back with a band I find in my purse. I continue sipping my drink while hiding behind the menu.

Interestingly, it turns out I'm close enough to hear them talking.

"It's really great to see you, buddy. I'm so glad we're getting a chance to do this." Lincoln's voice.

"I know. It's been forever since you've visited me down here. Do I have to remind you that you have free accommodation anytime you like?"

"No. It was just hard trying to coordinate Rachel's time off work, although that's not an issue now she's quit her job. But also, I didn't think you'd appreciate having two three-year-olds messing up your place."

"Actually, that's true. Sorry, Link, your daughters are adorable, but I have a lot of expensive shit at my house, and I don't want it damaged. I guess I'll just have to take you however I can."

"You haven't been to Brisbane for a while. Maybe you could come visit me?"

"It's funny you say that because I've been considering it recently. A gallery in Red Hill has mentioned doing an exhibition of some of my stuff."

"There you go. You can write it off as a tax deduction."

Their conversation is interrupted by the sound of a female voice.

"Lincoln Page? Oh my God. I'm a huge fan! I have loved you ever since you were on *Have You Got What It Takes?*" She then starts singing 'Roadhouse Blues', which was from his most famous performance back then.

"Uh, thanks," he says, sounding embarrassed as he cuts her off. "I'm just out having a drink with an old friend. But I appreciate you coming over to say hi."

I grin. He's even nice to the weird fans.

And then something occurs to me. *I* am one of the weird fans.

That's it. I'm going to have to leave.

I watch as a tall girl with long blonde hair appears from behind the partition. She pauses in front of me, talking loudly to someone on her phone. "Ayesha, guess who I've just been flirting with?"

A beat.

"Lincoln Page! You should totally come down to Nicky's Bar, and we'll all hang out. He has a cute friend too."

Another beat.

"Awesome. I'll see you in ten."

She totters off to order a drink, and I roll my eyes. But then I'm no better. Here I am, eavesdropping on Lincoln like a total stalker.

I'm not proud of myself.

"Do you think she knew we could hear her?" Felix asks.

"I don't know. But we should probably leave before her friend arrives. I'm obviously not interested in her, and I'm sure you're not in the mood for turning down a woman either."

"I didn't realise you were so famous, Link. You have groupies now?"

Lincoln laughs. "God, I hope not. Hey, I'm just going to settle the tab, and then we'll move on to somewhere else, okay?"

"Sounds good."

Finally. They'll be leaving in a minute, and I can put this whole sorry incident behind me.

I start composing a text to Millicent, telling her my predicament. She'll get a laugh out of my stupidity.

But then I sense the presence of someone standing in front of me, and I look up.

Uh-oh.

"I thought that was you! I'd recognise that hair anywhere."

Damn it. What kind of a bar is this when it's so bright someone can spot a person by their hair colour?

"Oh, hi. How funny that you're here too."

"I know! What are the odds? How was your meeting?"

"Better than expected actually. You?"

"Same! I probably shouldn't talk too much about it until it's all official, but I was *very* happy with the outcome."

"I'm so glad!"

"Wait here a minute. I'll be back."

I nod automatically. As if I wouldn't do anything Lincoln Page asked of me.

He disappears and returns a moment later with Felix. "Dude, this woman makes the most amazing stuff. She's an artist like you!" He motions to my phone. "Show him those photos you showed me."

"I'm not an *actual* artist."

"What you do is art," he says firmly. "Please. Show him."

I nervously open the photo gallery. Felix glances down at the images. Then rips the phone out of my hand to look at them more closely.

"Link's right. This *is* art. Wow." He studies me for a moment. "I love your look. I've decided we have to be friends. Link, she's mine now."

He laughs. "Whatever makes you feel better about yourself, buddy."

Felix grabs my arm. "We're ditching this place before a couple of ladies come back to throw themselves at a practically married man and a gay one. But I insist you come with us. I want to know everything about you."

"No, no. I don't want to impose." I almost say I know they don't get to catch up very often, but then it would be obvious I was listening in on their conversation.

"You're not imposing. We invited you. It would be rude to say no."

I know this isn't going to end well for me, but it's physically impossible to refuse.

"In that case, thank you. I would love to hang out with you both."

I sneak a peek at Lincoln. He seems completely at ease with me tagging along.

Felix ushers me out ahead of him, and we all leave the bar.

Tonight, I need to be on my best behaviour.

CHAPTER 6

LINCOLN

*T*he three of us walk farther along the wharf, and I have to say, I'm really enjoying myself. Seeing Felix was exactly what I needed, and running into Tash again was a happy coincidence.

Tash turns to me. "I talked to Daisy tonight, and she was so happy when I told her I got your autograph."

"I'm glad such a simple thing can make an impact," I say. "Is Daisy with her dad while you're away?"

"Uh, no. Her dad isn't around. He left before she was born."

I furrow my brow. "I'm sorry to hear that."

"It's okay. I'm glad he did it early on, rather than leave later."

"I guess." I never understood how fathers could abandon their kids like that, but I'm not going to make Tash feel any worse than I'm sure she already does.

"Anyway, to answer your question, Daisy is staying with my friend Missy. She has a little boy the same age as Daisy, and she's also on her own. But her ex is quite demanding with the custody arrangements, and he's always taking Ryder on these slightly terrifying outings, like mountain biking and ATV trekking. It really stresses Missy out because her ex isn't the most responsible of people."

"That sucks. But good that the dad is involved, I suppose."

We stop in front of a Mexican restaurant. "Are you hungry?" Felix asks.

"I could eat," I say.

"Actually, that's the reason I was at Nicky's but then I forgot to order," Tash says awkwardly. "So yes, let's do it."

As soon as we sit down, Felix orders a jug of sangria. "You want some?" he asks Tash.

"I won't say no. Hey, I read somewhere that the name sangria comes from the Spanish word for blood, which is *sangre.*"

"That's a fun fact *I* always tell people!" Felix says, delighted. "See, I already know we're going to be besties." He grabs her hand and kisses it playfully.

Tash orders some nachos. I order a vegetarian burrito, and Felix orders some quesadillas.

"Are you vegetarian?" Tash asks me.

"Yep. Almost ten years."

"For ethical reasons?"

"That's right."

"Ah." She looks like she might regret having ordered a meat dish.

"I'm totally fine with whatever anyone else wants to eat though," I assure her.

"I'm not turning veggie for you, sorry, Link," Felix says.

I laugh. "I don't expect you to. I would obviously be happy if more people ate less meat, but it's a personal decision that you have to arrive at yourself."

"Are your girls vegetarian?" Tash asks.

"Mostly. Rachel isn't though, and the girls wouldn't understand why they can't eat the same food as her, so I don't push it. I figure I'll be able to explain my reasoning to them once they get a bit older, and they can decide then. I don't agree with scaring children into doing something."

"I'm the same. I don't like using fear as a motivator."

The sangria arrives, and Felix pours us each a huge glass.

Tash downs half of hers in a couple of mouthfuls, and I raise an eyebrow. "Thirsty?"

She blushes. "I must be."

Felix looks at Tash thoughtfully. "If you don't mind me asking, do you have Japanese ancestry?"

Tash nods. "My mum's from a small town north of Tokyo. But my dad's family is from England."

"I love Japan. Have you been?"

"Yeah, a lot. I've visited my mum's family every couple of years for as long as I can remember. I even once lived there for a year. But my written Japanese is terrible, and my ability to speak it is very average. Have you visited recently?"

"The last time was three years ago. I spent five days in Tokyo, but I also went to Kyoto and Kanazawa."

"I love Kanazawa! The gardens are beautiful there." Tash turns to me. "What about you?"

I shake my head regretfully. "I haven't been yet, but I've always wanted to. Felix often talks about it."

"You should definitely go one day. I'm sure Felix will be able to advise you."

"Did you learn how to make those rice ball animals in Japan?" Felix asks.

"Not really. I mean, I got the idea from there, but I learned more from my mum, and websites and blogs while I lived here in Australia."

Our food arrives, and we all dig in. Tash must be hungry because she eats quickly.

Felix tops up our sangria. I don't usually get drunk, since I've seen what alcohol can do to a person, but I'm happy to indulge a little tonight.

"You should have made it to the final of *Sing to Me*," Tash tells me.

"It's okay. I'm actually kind of relieved. When you win, there's a lot of pressure to release your debut single immediately, and you don't get much input into the music on the album. That's what happened with *Have You Got What It Takes?* I was cast as this generic pop clone when I wanted to sing more stuff like what I've been doing now… rock and a little folk."

"Do you write your own music?" she asks.

"I do. But I haven't released any of it."

"Not even on YouTube or Soundcloud?"

"I've been telling him for years to get it out there," Felix cuts in. "But our boy is scared people won't like it."

"You can't hold back," Tash says. "Putting your dream out there is daunting, but you have to do it. If I hadn't taken the risk and tried to turn my hobby into a business, I'd still be working in an office making money for other people. This way, I'm doing what I love, and I have all the control."

"I know. But it's different with music. I've been playing small gigs since I was dropped by my record label, and I didn't feel like I was getting anywhere. That's why, when one of the producers invited me to audition for *Sing to Me*, I jumped at the chance."

"What were you singing at your gigs if you weren't playing your own stuff?"

"Just covers. Mostly the kind of stuff you heard me do on the show."

"Have you listened to any of his music?" she asks Felix.

"Nope."

"Has *anyone* heard your stuff?" she asks.

"Not really. I sing to my girls occasionally, but they love everything I do, so I obviously can't use them as an accurate gauge for commercial viability."

"Sing to us!" Felix begs.

I laugh. "No! We're having dinner, and those women over there are already staring."

Tash looks over to where four women are seated and giggling as they point at me. One of them makes eye contact with her and shoots her daggers. I frown.

"But how will you ever know whether you're any good unless you let other people hear you?" Felix points out.

"I can't trust *your* word, Felix," I say. "You'll only tell me what I want to hear."

"I promise I won't. And Tash will be honest." He gives her a pointed look. "Won't you?"

"Uh…"

"Traitor," Felix says. "You're supposed to say yes."

I smile, amused at Tash's inability to assure objectivity. She blushes again and drinks more sangria.

We finish eating, and Felix attempts to top up Tash's glass. She refuses.

"I should go back to my hotel," she says, hiccupping. "But thank you so much for inviting me out. It's nice to have company on a business trip."

"We'll walk you back," Felix says.

"No, no. You guys stay here. I'll be fine."

"I agree with Felix. We want to make sure you're safe," I say.

"Thank you. It's completely unnecessary, but I appreciate it."

We head to the door of the restaurant. Both Tash and I get out some cash, but Felix waves us away. "Let me."

"Please take my money," I say.

"Nope. I just sold a painting, so tonight is on me."

"You sure?"

"Yes. Completely."

"Thank you," Tash says.

"Felix is very talented," I tell her. "You'll have to look him up."

"What's your Instagram?" she asks him, getting out her phone.

"Felix Archer."

She finds him quickly and studies his images. "These are great! I'm following you right now."

Felix clicks a few buttons on his own phone. "And now I'm following you back. Your stuff is adorable."

We walk towards Tash's hotel, but Felix suddenly stops in the middle of the path.

"There's no one around. Sing now," he says to me.

I chuckle. "No!"

"If Lady Gaga can do it out the front of a convenience store, you can do it here."

"Um, that was a movie, not real life," I point out.

"I don't care. Sing us something. Please."

I turn to Tash with a pleading expression, but she grins. "I won't be the one saying you shouldn't."

I sigh. "Okay." I brush my hands through my hair. "You've put me on the spot. I can't think now!"

"Stop making excuses. Do it," Felix says.

"Fine."

I open my mouth and take a deep breath. I'm going to show them a song I wrote when I first met Rachel. At the time, I was listening to a lot of Incubus, so the vocal tone is similar to Brandon Boyd's.

You make me feel
Like I can do anything
You were under my skin
Way before I wanted to admit
But I'm glad you stayed
And fought for me.

I'm starting to relax into the chorus when the women from the restaurant spy us and rush over, squealing like deranged groupies.

I stop abruptly and smile politely at them.

Felix can sense my unease.

"Sorry, ladies. Show's over."

"No! We just got here. Sing 'Never Tear Us Apart!' one of them demands.

Felix grabs my arm and one of Tash's and starts striding away. "Next time," he calls over his shoulder.

The women continue protesting but thankfully don't follow us.

"That was a little intense," I say.

"But the song was great," Felix says.

I smile self-consciously. "I haven't quite worked out the ending yet."

"It was really, really good. Next time you play, you'll have to do a few of your own songs for sure."

"We'll see." I turn to Tash. "What did you think?"

"You should definitely sing your own stuff," she says quietly.

I beam. "Thanks."

We stop out the front of Tash's hotel. "It was so great hanging out with you guys," she says. "Thanks for letting me tag along tonight. And Lincoln, you'll need to do an all-ages show so I can bring Daisy."

"I'll work on it," I promise.

Felix gives her a kiss on each cheek. I'm a little more restrained with giving out affection to people I've just met, so I lightly squeeze her arm and smile.

"Bye."

She gives us one more quick wave and runs inside her hotel.

"I like her," Felix says.

"Yeah, she seems nice. I hope her business does well."

As we walk back to Felix's car, I reflect on the day. I can't believe I scored a national tour! It'll be exciting to go home and start preparing for it properly.

It occurs to me that Rachel never called back. I decide to leave it and see her tomorrow when I return to Brisbane.

I hate to admit it, but I'm on a high from a night spent with fun and supportive company, and I don't want to ruin it by talking to Rachel, who clearly wasn't in the most positive of moods earlier.

Reality will kick in soon enough.

CHAPTER 7

TASH

*B*ack home in Brisbane, everything feels fresh and exciting. I'm pumped from meeting Lincoln and Felix, but also from landing the biggest business deal of my career. There's a lot of work involved, but it'll be worth it in the long run.

The main thing is figuring out a smooth way to scale up production without affecting my existing customers. The chef I normally use already has a small team of helpers, and I work in the kitchen with him three days a week, but we're going to have to hire more people, and possibly expand our premises if we want to avoid any issues.

About once a month on a Friday night, I get my parents to look after Daisy so Millicent and I can hang out without the kids. Ryder's with his dad most weekends, from Friday after school until Sunday afternoon, so I know Millicent is nearly always free.

I let myself into her apartment around 6pm, not sure what the evening holds. I haven't dressed up, but Millicent and I are the same size, so I can always borrow her stuff if she decides we have to go somewhere fancy on a whim.

"Hey," I say, heading into the kitchen, where my bestie is pouring two glasses of sparkling wine.

"Hey, yourself," she says, handing me one.

"Is this fun wine or I-need-to-forget-about-the-week wine?" I ask.

She chuckles. "I guess fun wine. The week has been okay, although my boss is on at me to finish my current project. He doesn't realise how much work is involved. I swear he thinks I just type a bunch of random characters into my internet browser, and I'm suddenly inside the Reserve Bank's intranet."

Millicent's job sounds quite glamorous, but it's not. She's a professional hacker, hired by some obscure government department to test the strength of important websites. I'm in awe of her problem-solving abilities. The extent of my knowledge in technology is social media and working with my web developer on the online ordering side of my business. And even with those, I'm not particularly savvy.

"If you wanted, could you hack into a site that protected a bunch of money and steal it without anyone noticing?" I ask.

She laughs. "Of course. But it's still stealing. It wouldn't be any different than walking into a retail shop and taking a bunch of clothing without the assistant noticing."

"Yeah, I know. I guess I was thinking of those people who set up systems that divert a cent or two from a bunch of separate transactions into their own accounts, and then suddenly they're millionaires."

She shakes her head. "You watch too much TV."

I take a sip of my wine. "So what's the plan tonight? You want to stay in and watch a movie? Maybe overdose on chocolate?"

"Actually, yes. But first I've decided you need an online dating profile. I'm going to help you set one up."

"Wait, what? No! Don't I get a say in this?"

"'Fraid not, Tash. You haven't been on a date in forever! Apart from the obviously douchey move of ditching you while you were pregnant, Brad wasn't exactly the most romantic of people, and you were together, for what, a year? And then you were pregnant for nine months. Daisy's six now!"

"I'm well aware of my personal timeline, thank you."

"I'm just saying, you're thirty-five. You need to get back out there soon."

"You mean before I hit menopause?"

"No! That's not what I was getting at. Don't you get lonely sometimes?"

"Actually, no. I have Daisy and work and you. I really don't miss dating."

"That's probably because Brad was such a crappy partner. Imagine if you found someone nice. Someone like... Lincoln Page."

"If Lincoln Page happened to be single, then of course I would be interested. But he's not. Besides, I don't think it's fair to Daisy for me to start dating. She needs to know she has one person completely committed to her."

"Daisy will cope with you having a life. She's one of the most settled children I know. Also, you don't have to introduce anyone to her right away."

"I'm not sure, Missy. Online dating? Isn't that a bit lame?"

"No! That's the only real way to meet anyone now."

I raise an eyebrow. "How can that be? I swear when I was a teenager and the internet was starting to get big, it was considered nerdy and shameful to meet someone online."

She chuckles. "Times change, babe. Online is where it's at. Look!" She types something into her phone and shows me the screen. "This site's dedicated to serious prospects. There are others where you can just arrange a casual hookup if that's what you prefer."

"Is there an in-between?"

She frowns and types something else. "I guess this one might suit you. It's not all anonymous one-nighters, but I wouldn't say the members are looking for instant marriages either."

I sigh. "Okay, give me a look."

She hands me the phone, and I skim through a bunch of thumbnail images of apparently desirable single men.

"Are you supposed to swipe right or left?"

"Uh, right for yes, left for no."

I slow down and try to give each of the faces looking back at me the attention they deserve, but it's hard to judge someone by a still photo. "You know, when I first saw a picture of George Clooney, I couldn't understand the hype. But then I saw him in an actual movie, and I finally got it. It's his charisma and voice that contribute to the whole package. What happens if I miss out on one of these guys for the same reason?"

"Tash, you're overthinking things. Pick someone who looks nice, check out their bio, and swipe right to say you're interested. It's not rocket science."

"But it's turning dating into an emotionless game!"

"It's not. Try it and see. I swear you won't want to go back to the old-fashioned way once you get used to it."

"All right." I scroll through a dozen men, none of whom grab my attention. But then I pause on a guy with long, dark, curly hair.

Millicent peers over my shoulder and snorts. "You only like him because his hair vaguely resembles a certain reality singing star."

"So? Do you have a more scientific way of picking someone?"

"I guess not. If that's what turns you on, go for it. But you're logged in to my account. We'll need to set one up for you first."

I glance in the mirror mounted on the wall beside us. "I look hideous. You can't take a photo of me until I've done my hair and make-up."

"It doesn't work like that. You just link it to your social media account and then select some of the photos you've already uploaded."

"Oh. Okay."

"I think it's supposed to stop people from misrepresenting themselves completely. But of course we all know we're not always honest on social media."

"I am!"

"You are probably the only person in the universe who is."

She grabs my phone and sets up an account for me. "The guys are going to love you. You're an all-round hottie, and they're going to drool over your hair."

"Aw, thanks, sweetie."

She holds up a photo of me dressed in a red leather catsuit from her birthday last year. The party had a James Bond theme. "We could use this pic?"

"No!" I screech. "They'll think I'm into kinky stuff."

She chuckles. "You're right. That's not who you really are. How about this one?"

It's an image Millicent took of me when we were out to dinner last month. I'm wearing a tailored white shirt, showing just a hint of cleavage, and a pair of black slimline pants. Admittedly, I do look quite good there.

"All right. I give you permission to use that one."

"Excellent." She clicks a few more buttons. "Do you want me to fill out your bio?"

"Um, no thank you. I'll do that myself." I take a few minutes to write about my job and Daisy before showing Millicent.

"I wouldn't mention Daisy upfront," she warns.

"But I have to. Otherwise, it's false advertising!"

She rolls her eyes. "Then, at the very least, don't call yourself a mother. That's a huge turnoff. Write something like *I share custody of a six-year-old.*"

"Who am I sharing custody with?"

"It's too complicated to say you're a full-time working single mum, but your parents and best friend help you out with babysitting."

"Then what should I say?"

"Nothing! That kind of conversation should be had in person once you've already dazzled them with your charm."

"I don't know. It feels kind of deceitful."

"It's up to you. But I'm telling you, all you need to do on your profile is show them a little about who you are. They don't need to know *everything* all at once."

I go back and forth in my head, tossing up the pros and cons.

In the end, I decide Millicent might be right. And I justify my decision by thinking that at least I won't be attracting guys who might, heaven forbid, be interested in someone with a child for the wrong reasons.

"Okay. I'm going to take your advice."

"I think it's the right thing to do," she assures me. She finalises my account and then locates the guy I liked before, swiping his image into the interested group. "There. You've completed your first step into the world of online dating."

"Now what?"

"Pick a few others and wait to see if they like you back."

"What if I get multiple?"

"Then you can date all of them. Or none. It's up to you."

"This is *so* weird."

"It's no weirder than approaching a random stranger in a bar and hoping for the best. At least here, you get a bit of info about them beforehand."

"I guess."

My phone dings. I look at the screen and grin despite my earlier reservations.

"The guy with the hair likes me back!"

Millicent laughs. "See? I knew you'd get the appeal right away. Ask him out for a drink."

"Not a meal?"

"No. Pick somewhere not too far away, but not so close he'll be able to follow you home. And organise it so that if you don't like him, you can make a quick escape."

"Should I text you and get you to call me with a fake emergency?"

"You can be a grown-up about it if he's not what you're after. But if that's too hard, just tell him you have another appointment."

"Oh, okay." I tentatively type a message to my match. His name is Tomas. No H. "Do you think we should meet in the morning or afternoon?"

"I guess it depends on how eager he is to catch up. Maybe Sunday at 5pm? That keeps it casual. And then if you hit it off, you can stay out and go for dinner."

"That makes sense." I suggest to Tomas that we meet for a drink at a place on James Street.

He replies immediately.

Sounds good. I'll see you there.

I hold up the phone to show her. "Look!"

"See? Easy."

"Agh! What do I wear? What do I talk about? Are you able to look after Daisy?"

"Relax! Yes, of course I'll look after Daisy. And you have a ton of cute clothes. We'll figure this out. Also, I've never known you to be short for conversation topics. You'll be fine."

"Okay." I take a deep breath and let it out slowly. "You're right. I can do this."

CHAPTER 8

LINCOLN

I can't wait to get home and see the girls. As soon as I'm inside the door, I wrap them both up in a huge hug. "I missed you two little munchkins."

"We missed you too, Daddy. Can we get ice cream now?"

"Yes! Give me half an hour, and then we'll go."

Both girls give me an extra tight squeeze and run off, discussing the flavours they're going to order.

I find Rachel in the lounge, reading something on her phone.

"Hey!" I say, going over and giving her a kiss on the forehead. "I feel like I've hardly seen you lately."

"That's because you haven't," she says matter-of-factly.

I sit down beside her. "I'm sorry. I know this is all really crazy, but I'm going to try to make it work for everyone. I don't want you to feel like you're on your own, looking after the girls. In fact, I should have a lot more time now than when I was on the show, at least until the tour starts. And then after it finishes, I can basically dictate my own hours."

"I guess."

"Is that what's bothering you? I mean, you seemed

disappointed that I didn't get an international tour. If I had, that would have been a lot worse."

"But it would also have meant a lot more money. You're only going to be getting a little more than you were for your local gigs, but you'll be around less."

"I… I'm not sure what to say. Do you want me to pull out of the tour? I can just go get a regular nine-to-five job if that would be easier."

"And what would that make me, huh?" she snaps. "A dream-killer?"

"Hey, hey, no. We're a team here. We need to make sure you're happy too. Are you frustrated because you're not working?"

Rachel did three days a week in retail before I went on *Sing to Me*, but she gave it up once I made it past the audition round. I had to be at the studio most days, and Rachel never knew what her schedule was going to be like more than a few weeks in advance. The twins go to pre-school twice a week, but they're set days, so it used to be my responsibility to do the drop-off and pickup.

"No. I hated retail. But I guess I did like being able to contribute financially. Especially when your wage isn't really enough for us to live on."

"I haven't been sent the figures for this upcoming tour, but it sounds like it will be more than enough to keep us going, at least for the rest of the year."

"And then what?"

"I guess we wait and see what happens after that. If things get quiet, I'll pick up a few extra shifts at the café."

She drags her hands down her face. "I just hate not having any stability."

"We should talk about that. What do you need to feel stable?"

"Damn it. Why are you so calm and reasonable? You're making me seem like a crazy person!"

I stand. Rachel gets in moods like this every now and again.

All I can do is give her some space and then talk to her after she's had time to articulate her thoughts. "I'm going to unpack, and then I'll take the girls out. You're welcome to come too. We can finish the conversation then?"

"No, I think you should take them out on your own. Make up for all the time you've been away."

"Okay."

I head off to the bedroom, taking my suitcase with me.

While I love that woman, she can be hard work sometimes. But of course all relationships require patience and understanding. I'm probably tired from the events of the last few days. Weeks, even.

I'm sure everything will return to normal soon.

It's so good to get outside with the girls and just be a dad. I tie my hair back and wear a baseball cap to try to avoid having anyone recognise me, but most people are cool anyway. I notice a couple of passers-by do a double-take, but I think they keep their distance because I'm with my family.

I help the girls climb on the rope spiderweb at the South Bank playground, and we dip our toes in the water at the artificial beach. It's almost warm enough to go swimming, but I didn't think to bring our swimsuits. At least the twins don't mind walking around town. Normally, I wouldn't be able to get them to go for more than ten minutes at a time, but they suck it up, knowing that the end reward is their favourite gelato. I buy them each a cup: Isabella with strawberry, and Madison with salted coconut and mango salsa. Madison has always been the more adventurous of the two girls.

We sit in the corner of the store looking out the window, and I think about my conversation with Rachel earlier. I really have no idea what to do. I wonder if there's something else bothering her that she's not saying. I know she grew up without a lot of money, but she's never complained about our lack of funds before. The girls have never gone without anything, and while I guess we can't afford fancy overseas trips or a big house, we get by. At least we own our place, and we don't have a huge mortgage. I bought the property when I got 'famous' the first time. It was probably the smartest thing I've ever done.

I'll just have to keep Rachel up to date with all the tour plans and make sure she feels like she's being heard. If she wants to go and study for a new career or get another job, we'll make that work.

※

WE HEAD HOME a couple of hours later, and I find Rachel still on the couch.

"I want to apologise for earlier," I say.

She gives me a small smile. "I'm sorry too. I know I sounded like a spoilt brat, but life has been kind of tough lately. I feel like I'm losing myself."

"You have the strongest identity of nearly anyone I know, Rach. There's no way you'll ever fade into the background."

She holds out her arms, and I sink into them.

"You always know the right thing to say."

"I try. But we'll figure out a solution so you feel like you're also getting your needs met. Do you want to do some study? Or get a different job?"

"I'll think about it and get back to you."

The girls see us hugging and run over to jump on top.

"Sandwich hug!" I call out. The girls squish into the middle, and we stay like that for ages.

This is my happy place.

CHAPTER 9

TASH

I'm not sure about this dating thing.

I'm standing outside the bar waiting for Tomas, and I've almost changed my mind and left about twenty times in the last five minutes. I probably shouldn't have gotten here so early. The whole fashionably late thing never felt quite right, but it would have helped my nerves this afternoon.

I fiddle with my earrings and check my reflection in the window, smoothing down my hair. I decided to keep my outfit simple, with a white shell top, a long yellow chiffon skirt, and strappy gold heels.

As I'm contemplating an escape again, he appears. He's shorter than I expected, and his hair is nothing like Lincoln's in real life. While Lincoln's is thick and ringlety, this guy's is kind of thin and straggly. Still, that's not his fault. I shouldn't be so judgy.

He smiles when he sees me. "Hi. Natasha?"

I paste on a smile in return. "Yes. Hi. Tomas."

He comes over and gives me a kiss on both cheeks. He smells quite strongly of cheap lime-scented aftershave, and thanks to the double kiss, he has now transferred the fragrance to me.

"After you," he says, ushering me into the bar. "What would you like to drink?"

"I think I'll get a mojito." I figure they have lime in them, which might distract me from the amount on my skin. I swear it's getting stronger.

"Why don't you grab a seat, and I'll bring it over?"

"Thank you." I rummage around in my purse and pull out a twenty to cover my drink. "Here's some money."

He takes it. "Thanks."

I find a couple of stools in the corner and nervously sit down. Tomas is standing at the bar, laughing at something the woman behind the counter is saying. Apart from his hair, which really isn't that bad, and the lime overload, he seems okay so far. He's wearing a loose pair of chinos and a long-sleeved black shirt.

He comes over with the drinks and puts the mojito in front of me. I take a big sip to calm my jitters.

"Have you met many people on dating sites?" I ask.

He laughs. "A few. Why? Do you want a list?"

"No, no. Sorry. I was just making conversation. You're the first person I've met on one."

He raises an eyebrow. "Really? You're a dating-site virgin?"

I'm not sure I like the way he said the word *virgin*, but I'll give him the benefit of the doubt.

"I, uh, I guess I'm a bit out of practice with the whole dating thing in general." Now would be the time to tell him about Daisy, but for some reason I hesitate.

"That's okay. I find that refreshing actually. There are a lot of crazy and jaded women out there."

"I suppose there'd be a lot of douchebags those women have to deal with," I point out.

He frowns. "Are you a feminist?"

I swallow, a little taken aback. "I'm not sure what prompted you to ask that, but if you mean, do I think all women should be treated equally to men? Then, yes."

"All the feminists I know go on about 'toxic masculinity' and group all men in as part of the #MeToo movement."

This went in a very strange direction very fast. "It's more complex than that. Maybe not something you want to get into two minutes after meeting some–"

He cuts me off. "I'm sick of women blaming all men for their problems. We're not the enemy, you know!"

I look at him, bewildered. "I never said you were."

"How am I responsible for some random guy raping a woman?"

"Uh, you're not?" Jeez, this guy has a massive chip on his shoulder.

"Yeah, but that's not what all those feminists think. They say we have to take responsibility. For what, I don't fucking know."

This is not going at all how I planned. And if I really wanted to, I could try to explain that being a part of any demographic that negatively affects another doesn't mean you are directly responsible, but you do have a duty as a decent human being to listen to the people speaking out and see if there's anything you can do to help the situation. But I don't think he'd appreciate that.

"Maybe I should leave," I say, starting to stand.

It's like he doesn't even hear me. "I should have known. Any woman with fluoro hair is either gay or a left-wing feminist."

Okay. That's definitely enough.

"I'm going to go."

I hurry out, annoyed that I didn't get to finish my drink, and head around the corner to order an Uber to take me home.

What the actual hell? How could I have misjudged the situation so badly?

If this is what online dating is like, I'm going to be single for the rest of eternity.

MILLICENT'S DISTURBED to see me home so early.

"What happened? What did you do?"

"Why did you think it was something *I* did? Tomas was a freakin' weirdo. I swear, within two seconds of us sitting down, it was like he was reading directly from a textbook for woman haters."

"Oh no."

"Yes! I actually think he might require medication. There was something really wrong with the guy."

"I'm sorry, Tash. We probably should have looked at his bio more closely. I just didn't want to freak you out when you were already a bit wary of the whole experience."

She opens her phone and navigates to Tomas's page on the dating site.

"Ah, see. I should have known. He's written here that he likes upbeat women."

"And that means he's a raving misogynist?"

"Yep. It assumes that women should always be happy specifically for their partner. Other things to look out for are when a guy says he wants someone who 'looks after themselves' because you know that's code for 'if you don't starve yourself or go to the gym seven days a week, don't even think about coming near me.' Or if their pic shows them on a large motorcycle, you know they're overcompensating for something."

"I'm not going out with anyone else from online."

"But you have to! Don't let one bad guy mess up your chance for happiness."

"What if I tried something else? Maybe I could find someone in one of those meet-up groups instead. You know, the kind where they all go hiking or surfing?"

"Do you know who goes to meet-up groups? People over sixty. Come on, Tash. Give online dating another try."

"I'll have to think about it. But right now, I want to get into my PJs and watch old reruns of *How I Met Your Mother*. At least that show never lets me down."

Millicent sighs. "Okay. Sorry, hon. I really just want you to be happy."

"I know. And I appreciate you helping me. But I think meeting someone is something I have to do on my own. On my terms."

"You want me to stay tonight?"

"It's up to you. If Ryder's already settled then you might as well."

"I've got the kids set up in Daisy's room with the iPad. They're watching the Disney Channel."

"Maybe leave them then. You feel like laughing at some of Barney's antics with me?"

"Yeah, why not. My love life isn't exactly happening right now either."

"Have you met many guys online?"

"That's the *only* way I meet them. But it does seem to be getting harder and harder to find the nice ones. There's so much ghosting and... what's that other thing they do? Zombie-ing? You know, where they totally ignore you, but then three months later they suddenly start liking your social media posts? I don't get that at all. Oh, and then there's catfishing. Thank God I've never had to deal with that..."

I shake my head. "And you thought I would benefit from entering this world?"

"It's worth it in the long run. If you look up the stats, at least a third of people online are looking for serious relationships. And like, ten per cent of people end up getting married."

"Is that ten per cent of the third or the total?"

"I don't know. Does it matter?"

"It would probably be a big difference in figures."

"Either way, there are good guys out there. You just have to kiss a few frogs first."

I'm starting to wonder if that's true. Is there really another guy out there for me? Or are all the eligible ones already taken?

But then Ted on *How I Met Your Mother* took forever to find his match. Maybe I'll have to wait a bit longer. Although I hope I don't have to take as many detours as he did to end up with 'the one'.

Love might be a bit more trouble than it's worth.

CHAPTER 10

LINCOLN

*P*laying music with my guys is one of the best things in the world. And while live performances are the ultimate, I can relax and enjoy myself a lot more with rehearsals. We're currently practising a bunch of songs in Beau's garage. He's the band's drummer and lives outside the city in a large property so we don't have to worry about disturbing any neighbours.

It's Saturday, and exactly nine weeks until we start the tour. I'm looking forward to getting out of south-east Queensland to play in the other states and perform at some bigger venues. Normally we play pubs and small clubs, but this time we'll be doing actual concert halls.

Things have calmed down at home over the last couple of months. Rachel hasn't mentioned feeling left out or ignored – and she seems happy enough, so I'm quietly optimistic that she feels our lives are headed in a positive direction. Occasionally I've tried to prompt her about whether she wants to enrol in a course or fill out any job applications but she hasn't seemed particularly interested. Maybe she's realised that the money I'm going to be earning for the tour is enough for us after all.

I start playing a few chords on my guitar, ones that go with the song I sang for Felix and Natasha that night in Sydney. They probably don't realise, but their positive reaction has inspired me to get more serious about my songwriting.

Jesse, the lead guitarist, joins in, and then Andy, the bassist, takes his cue. Finally, Beau starts tapping out a beat. And it works. I quietly sing the lyrics so the guys can hear what I initially intended for the song.

Afterwards, they all look at me, surprised. "Where did that come from?" Beau asks.

"I wrote it a while back but I didn't want to push my stuff on you in case you didn't like it."

"Dude! We've been dropping hints to do originals for years! We always thought you wanted to stick with covers because they were easy."

"I guess that's true in a way. But I've kind of realised lately that I need to take more risks." I think back to my conversation with Natasha about how she pursued her dream – and at the time, I made excuses for why I couldn't pursue mine. But it was bullshit. I was just scared. Going on *Sing to Me* helped me remember I have talent, but that night in Sydney confirmed I should be following my dreams more fully.

"Then let's do something with it. Talk to Max and see if he'll let us test out a couple of tunes on the tour. And obviously reassure him we'll still do the fan favourites."

"Okay, I will. And of course, if any of you have songs you want to try, let me know."

They all look at each other with an expression I can't decipher.

"What?"

Beau answers. "We kind of started working on some stuff while you were on the show. We were going to tell you at some point, but then Max gave us the tour, and we didn't want to complicate things further."

"You should have said! I'd love to hear what you've come up with!"

Beau looks relieved. "Great. Do you want to go through some of them now?"

I check the time. It's already 4pm. Wow. That went fast. We've been here for over four hours.

"Actually, I better head home. Rachel will be wondering what happened to me. But I definitely want to hear what you've got at the next rehearsal."

"No problem," Jesse says. "I'll set up a share drive for us so we can store all our files."

"Awesome."

I nod at the guys and head out to the car, lugging my amp, guitar and microphone with me.

I sing in the car all the way home. I can't believe we're finally branching out into originals. And even if Max doesn't want us to play them on tour, it shouldn't stop us from experimenting in our own time. It's crazy that the whole band was so worried about rocking the boat that we never really talked about trying something new.

But for now, that can wait, because I'm looking forward to a relaxed evening at home with my girls. I need to make the most of it while I can. Rachel hasn't confirmed whether she and the twins are going to accompany me for part of the tour yet, but I have a feeling she won't want to come along for much of it.

I pull into the driveway, taking all my stuff in with me. It's not cheap equipment, so I can't afford to leave it in the car out on the street.

"Hello?" I call out as I dump everything just inside the door.

Silence.

"Anyone home?"

Still no answer.

I curiously peek inside the living room and the girls' bedroom but don't find them. They must have gone out somewhere. I dial Rachel's number, and it goes to voicemail.

Weird.

I make myself a coffee and sit at the kitchen bench. It'll be 5pm soon. Rachel never usually has the girls out past six unless it's a special occasion. I'll start planning dinner, and I'm sure they'll be home before I know it.

I should probably have a shower first though. Singing and playing guitar in a garage for several hours can be hot work.

After stripping off my shirt, I'm about to throw it in the washing basket when I pause at the edge of the walk-in closet. Something doesn't look right.

It takes a moment for me to realise that Rachel's side is almost completely empty. I open her drawers and notice nearly everything is gone from there too.

A sinking feeling settles in my chest. Of course she might have taken everything out to do a spring clean, but when I look up at the top shelf and notice a couple of suitcases are also gone, my heart starts racing.

This *cannot* be happening.

I bolt over to the girls' room and rip open their closet. It's almost empty as well.

What's Rachel done?

I scour the house for a note but am unable to find one. I have no idea who to call. The police? But what if it's all just a dumb misunderstanding? Did Rachel have a pre-planned getaway I forgot about?

No, that's definitely not the case. Of course I'd remember if my partner and children were going away.

I don't want to face the possibility that she's left me. It doesn't make sense. Has she been blackmailed or kidnapped? Our life was so good. Sure, she seemed a bit moody after I didn't win *Sing to Me*, but we were happy most of the time.

I'm very, very confused. And scared.

I do another quick check of the house. Where would they have gone? Most of Rachel's family live in the UK, and she doesn't have a lot of close friends here in Brisbane. At least, none that would accommodate two young girls. And most of her acquaintances are younger than her and childless. Their lives are all about their careers and partying.

That's it. I'm phoning the police.

I'm just dialling the number when my phone beeps.

It's a text from Rachel.

I open it.

Holy shit.

CHAPTER 11

TASH

*I*t's only three weeks until my meals start being stocked in supermarkets. I'm equally excited and terrified. What if they completely flop? Or what if they're super successful, and I run out of stock in the first few days? Obviously the latter outcome would be preferable, but I want the team who approved the deal to see how professional I am and feel they made the right decision.

I can't believe it's been ten weeks since that first meeting in Sydney. It feels like no time's passed, but also an eternity.

That's also how long it's been since I met Lincoln, and I have to say, my crush on him has not abated in the slightest. I check his Instagram feed every day, hoping he posts a new selfie I can drool over or provide a little further insight into his personal life. But in a way, how I feel about him now is more the way I'd feel about any attractive celebrity – a sort of pretend fantasy with my own ideals projected onto him. If I met him again, I'd probably be disappointed by how little he resembles what I've built up in my head.

He finally posted about his secret news, and it turns out he's going on a national tour. I am *so* buying a ticket for that show, even if I have to go alone.

It's Monday morning, and I've just arrived back home after dropping Daisy at school. I make myself a cup of tea and sit down to look through my Instagram feed. Felix has a gorgeous new artwork that vaguely resembles a close-up of lilies, painted in a rainbow of vivid blues, greens and oranges. He and I regularly comment on each other's posts with supportive messages. It's a shame he lives in Sydney because I think we'd hang out all the time in person otherwise.

The other people I follow are mostly acquaintances posting shots of their weekend adventures. I click the small heart icon beside most of them and then go to the search function. Lincoln's name is at the top, as usual. I still haven't summoned the courage to officially follow him, but if he was able to see his account stats, he'd discover I was one of his top fans.

A mix of emotions flows through me when I see his most recent post. It's a black square with white text that reads Betrayal shows up where you least expect it.

What does that mean? Has JC's manager cancelled the tour? That would be a pretty big betrayal, considering what happened the first time he made it in the music industry.

I scroll to the comments. Lincoln hasn't written a caption underneath, but dozens of his followers have posted messages.

Are you OK?

I'm sorry to hear you're going through a tough time. My thoughts are with you.

What's wrong?

Is your tour still on?

And then I see a message from Felix. He should have learned from last time, but apparently not.

Hang in there, buddy. I'll see you soon.

I wonder if that means he's coming to Brisbane, or if Lincoln's going to visit him. I so badly want to contact Lincoln, but it doesn't seem right. I only really spoke to him for a few hours over two and a half months ago.

I send a screenshot of the post to Millicent.

Look what Lincoln posted on IG. What do you think it means?

She types back. I don't know. Probably just some vague-posting to boost his profile. Maybe lyrics to a new song?

Me: But Felix said he's going to see him. There might be something wrong.

Millicent: There's nothing you can do if there is.

I sort of agree with her but it seems weird not even offering condolences if something bad happened.

Me: You're right. I'm just being a crazy stalker again.

Millicent: You are. Now go do some work. Or get back on that dating site and expend all that sexual energy on someone you're actually allowed to sleep with.

I post the emoji with the tongue sticking out as a way of ending the conversation.

I might just send a quick message to Felix. There's no harm in enquiring after someone's well-being.

After careful consideration, I write, *Hey Felix! I hope you're well. Have you spoken to Lincoln recently? I just wanted to check he's all right after that post he put on Instagram – but I didn't want to bother him directly. Please pass on my best wishes. Tash.*

I spend the next half hour trying to focus on work, but I'm not very successful. I'm supposed to be liaising with the supermarket chain's marketing department so we can finish organising advertising for my meals, but every time I start browsing through my photo gallery to look for appropriate images, my thoughts wander back to Lincoln.

Finally, my phone dings with a notification from Felix.

> Hey, chicky. I don't know the full story yet, but I'll
> be in Brisbane tomorrow afternoon. I'll contact
> you on Wednesday morning if that's OK?

I write back that I look forward to hearing from him.

I hope Lincoln's all right.

It doesn't sound like he was just posting lyrics to a new song.

&

I CAN BARELY CONCENTRATE at all for the next couple of days, although I know I need to keep working hard. Slacking on my dream while waiting to talk to a friend about my celebrity crush would be stupid.

However, I still wake up at five on Wednesday morning, unable to stay asleep. I make sure my phone is charged and the volume is turned up, and I even leave it within a few feet of the shower while I wash my hair.

I don't pay attention while I'm preparing Daisy's lunch, and I accidentally make her a peanut butter sandwich, even though her school has a total nut ban. For the record, she doesn't like me making really elaborate food for her every day, and sometimes she just wants a plain cheese sandwich and store-bought cookies like her friends.

Felix finally contacts me at 10am, by which time I've refreshed both his and Lincoln's Instagram feeds at least a dozen times each. I know this isn't the behaviour of a normal person but I'm unable to stop.

When the message comes through, I dive on my phone.

> Hey, Tash. I'm making Lincoln come with me to
> the Muschalla Gallery in Red Hill this morning.
> You want to join us?

Do I want to go with them? Ha! If I wrote back how badly I

did actually want to join them, I'd probably scare them off forever. So instead, I write,

> I'd love to, but are you sure? Will Lincoln mind?

Felix: Lincoln isn't capable of much rational thought right now. I could use the extra support.

Uh-oh. That definitely doesn't sound good.

> Me: OK. When are you leaving? I'll meet you there.

Felix: 45 minutes?

> Me: Sounds good. See you soon.

Poor Lincoln. Something really bad must have happened if Felix is talking like that.

I dress in some white jeans and a faded denim shirt, thinking I need to look – and act – like a supportive friend, rather than an insane groupie.

I tie my hair into a bun and head out the door, my heart thumping. Who knows what kind of situation I'm about to encounter?

I live in Highgate Hill in an old-fashioned Queenslander, and there's a bus stop just outside my door. I own a car but due to the lack of free parking around the city it's usually more convenient to take public transport. I'm just deciding whether I should take my car when a bus pulls up. That answers my question. I jump on and scan my pass.

§

HALF AN HOUR LATER, I arrive at the Muschalla Gallery and nervously head inside.

Felix and Lincoln are already in there, but they're facing the other way, looking at a gorgeous painting by a local indigenous artist.

The floor is polished timber, so they turn when they hear my footsteps. Felix's face lights up, and he hurries over to give me a hug. "Hey! It's good to see you again."

"You too! Thanks for inviting me." I anxiously peer over his shoulder at Lincoln. His face is expressionless. Felix follows my gaze and whispers in my ear. "Don't take it personally if he seems a little distant. He's been through a lot these past few days."

I tentatively make my way over to where he's standing. "Hi. I hope you don't mind me tagging along. Felix said it was okay, but if you need some space…"

He gives me a small tired smile. "No, please stay. The more distraction the better right now."

I figure I'll find out what's wrong soon enough, so I make it my mission to lighten the mood as much as possible.

"I love the paintings here," I say to Felix. "Are any of them yours?"

"No but I hope to soon have some on display. Not that I need a reason to come and visit my buddy in his hometown, but I thought I'd kill two birds with one stone and talk to the gallery owner." Felix tilts his head towards the back of the room, where a tall woman with a blonde bob is headed for us. "Speak of the devil." He approaches the woman and kisses her hand. "It's lovely to finally meet you in person, Deirdre."

"Likewise." She smiles politely at Lincoln and me. "I see you've brought a couple of friends."

"Yes, but they'll entertain themselves while I chat with you." He lightly squeezes my arm. "Why don't you take my boy for a coffee and meet me back here in half an hour?"

I panic. I thought the three of us were going to hang out together. I am wholly unprepared to be alone with a depressed Lincoln Page.

Lincoln nods. "Cool. Text me if you're done earlier." He then looks at me. "Have you been to Channing's around the corner?"

"Actually, yes. They have really good chai."

He points to the door, ushering me out first. "A chai and a slice of their fig-and-almond tart sounds really good."

Lincoln obviously needs a friend.

I force myself to relax. It's all going to be fine. I can do this.

CHAPTER 12

LINCOLN

Inside Channing's, Tash makes me stay put while she orders the chai and tart. She then sits back down and looks at me. I avoid her gaze and stare out the window.

"How's... how's your music going?" she asks.

I wave a hand. "Fine."

"So the tour's still on?"

I nod, my mouth set in a straight line.

"Is that a bad thing?" she asks.

"No, it's a good thing," I say flatly.

"You don't seem very happy about it," she points out gently.

"It's kind of hard to muster the energy to be excited when the reason you were doing all this in the first place is gone."

She frowns. "I'm sorry, but what does that mean?"

I cover my face and let out a shaky breath. Tash quickly comes over to my side of the table and wraps an arm around me, rubbing my back. It's a sweet gesture, but it almost tips me over the edge.

The waiter puts our drinks and food on the table, but I ignore them.

"Do you want to leave?" Tash asks quietly.

I sniff and shake my head. "God, I'm sorry about that. I'm never like this in public. Please, sit down, and we'll wait for Felix."

"You don't have to apologise for being upset. Would it help if you talked about it?"

"Probably not. But I'm grateful you're keeping me company so you deserve to know." I reach into my pocket and pull out my phone, handing it to her. "Open the last message from Rachel."

Tash narrows her eyes but does as I say.

The words are seared on my brain.

> I'm sorry to do this to you, Link, but I couldn't live a lie anymore. We both deserve better. I'm going to London with the girls to live with my parents. I hope one day you can forgive me.

Tash looks up at me, mouth agape. "What happened? She can't just leave the country with your daughters without permission, can she?"

I stare at her, my eyes stinging with the effort to hold in tears. "Apparently she can. Because it turns out they're not biologically mine."

She gasps. "What the actual hell?"

I snort a bitter chuckle. "My sentiments exactly."

"But that's… that's outrageous! How can someone do that to another person? How can she do that to *you*? You're the sweetest guy ever!"

I feel my face soften. "You don't know me very well but I appreciate you saying so."

"You were on reality TV twice, and I saw you both times. I know they say the footage on those shows is heavily manipulated but I could still tell what you were like. I know when someone's only giving the impression of being nice and when they're genuine. You're the real deal."

I take a sip of chai and then say, "You're very kind. I'm glad Felix invited you today."

"Can you take Rachel to court? Force her to let you see the girls?"

"I don't know. I haven't talked to a lawyer yet. This only happened the other day so I'm still getting my head around it."

"Did she say who the father is?"

"Yeah. I finally got some information out of her once she landed in London. He's some childhood sweetheart who lives near her parents over there. She told me they slept together once on a trip we did a while back. There was this one night where she told me she was going out with a bunch of old girlfriends, and she didn't want me along, saying I'd be bored. But instead she hooked up with him."

"How can she be sure he's the father?"

"She had a paternity test done." I clench my hands together. "And you know how long ago she knew?"

Tash doesn't say anything.

"Before the girls were even fucking born! She had one of those diagnostic things done at twelve weeks! She's been lying to me for *four* years!"

"I'm so sorry, Lincoln. That's truly, truly horrible."

We sit in silence for a while. I nibble at my tart but I'm not hungry. I feel bad dragging Tash into this mess. She doesn't need to be a part of it.

My phone beeps. I glance at the screen. "Felix is done. We should go back."

She nods. We head outside and walk slowly back to the gallery. "Do you live nearby?" she asks. "I'm over in Highgate Hill."

"I'm just in Ashgrove. Only about ten minutes away."

"Well, I just want to say if you ever need anything, or if you want to hang out with me and my crazy friend Millicent, you're always welcome."

"Thank you. That means a lot. I have to admit, I don't have a lot of close friends anymore. When I wasn't playing gigs or working at a friend's café, most of my time was taken up with Rachel and the girls."

"I'm sure you have a bigger support network than you realise. But either way, it might be nice to spend time with people not associated with your inner circle."

"Exactly."

We get back to the gallery, and Felix is waiting outside. He looks pleased, but I can see him toning down the enthusiasm for my sake. I feel guilty that I'm ruining what would otherwise be a good day for him.

"How did you go?" I ask.

"Great. They're going to do an exhibition in a few months."

"That's awesome." I force a smile to show I'm really happy for him.

"What do you want to do now?" he asks. "Go out for lunch somewhere?"

I run my hands through my hair. "Actually, if it's okay, do you mind dropping me at home? I'm sure Tash will be much better company."

"I don't want to leave you alone," Felix protests. "You need to be mingling in society."

"I didn't sleep well last night so I'd prefer to go home and take a nap."

Felix looks dubious but can see I'm not going to change my mind. "All right. Tash and I will get something to eat, and I'll bring leftovers back to your place."

I smile weakly. "Thanks."

"Did you want to leave your car here, and I can bring you back later?" Felix asks Tash.

"Oh, I caught the bus, so I can do whatever."

"Perfect. My ride's over here." He points to a sleek silver Audi rental parked near the kerb and waves at the passenger side. "I'll let you two fight it out for shotgun."

"I'll sit in the back," I say immediately.

"No, no. You take the front," Tash says.

"Too late." I open the back door and slide in.

She gives me a stern look through the window but I pretend not to notice.

She hops in the front seat. "Thank you, Lincoln."

"My pleasure."

CHAPTER 13

TASH

*I*t's so weird, but I've gone from feeling like a starstruck groupie to an overprotective friend in the space of an hour. I just want Lincoln to feel better.

Felix turns the key in the ignition and types something into his phone. Within seconds, one of Lincoln's performances from *Sing to Me* is blaring over the speakers. It's a cover of 'Wicked Game' by Chris Isaak. I thought it was amazing at the time but I wonder if it's a bit melancholy.

Lincoln seems to agree with me. "Turn that shit off," he growls.

"Sorry, I just really love that song." Felix changes the music. Soon, the Arctic Monkeys are singing 'Why'd You Only Call Me When You're High?' instead. I suppose that's a slight, if not random, improvement.

We drive silently across to Ashgrove and down a quiet leafy street. Only it's not so quiet when we get near a contemporary-looking house with a big jacaranda tree out the front. There are at least six cars parked on the road and in the driveway. It takes a second before I realise there are also several people standing around with microphones and cameras.

"Lincoln, get down," I order.

He must see what I've seen and obeys without argument.

"What the hell?" Felix asks as we slow down.

"Keep going!" I tell him. "Don't stop."

Felix speeds up again, and we quickly pass the crowd. Thankfully Lincoln doesn't live in a dead-end street, so we don't have to double back.

"It looks like the paparazzi have discovered where you live," I say, turning to face him. "You can't go back there, so you're coming to my place. We'll figure out your next move there."

"I don't want to put you out," Lincoln says quietly.

"You're not putting me out. No one deserves to have the media following them around. Especially with your current situation."

"What do you think they wanted?" Felix asks as I direct him to my place.

"It's the paparazzi. They want photos that'll make them money. But we're not going to give them anything."

We arrive at my house, and I get Felix to park in the driveway.

After unlocking the door, I usher them inside. I'm not the tidiest of people, but thankfully I did a clean-up this morning with all my nervous energy.

The guys follow me through to the lounge, where I point at the couch. "Take a seat while I make some food." The kitchen is only separated by a small counter, so I can still talk to them.

"Please don't go out of your way for us," Lincoln insists.

"I'd be making myself something anyway, so it's no trouble."

I get out some flour, eggs, tempura crumbs and cabbage. "Are you okay with eggs and dairy?" I ask Lincoln.

"Yes, thanks. What are you making?"

"Okonomiyaki. Have you ever had it before?"

"I haven't, no."

"Seriously, Link, you are going to love it," Felix cuts in. "We really need to expand your palate. They sell okonomiyaki everywhere now."

He smiles sadly. "The girls didn't handle late nights very well, so we didn't really go out for dinner that much. And I guess whenever we went out during the day, it was to the park, and we'd take a packed lunch."

"I don't get out much either," I tell Lincoln. "Millicent and I try to have a kid-free night once a month, but we often just stay in and binge-watch TV."

Lincoln stares bleakly at the wall. "I can't handle the idea of starting over. And not seeing my girls..." He breaks down and Felix comes to the rescue. I continue cooking, hoping my food will distract him for a few minutes.

I have a little rice left over from last night, so after I've put the first okonomiyaki in the frying pan, I cut up some seaweed and shape two balls to look like pandas. I put each of them on a small plate and carry them over to the coffee table, placing them down in front of the guys.

Felix picks one up and inspects it. "Oh my God, I love these! Link, aren't they fantastic?"

Lincoln musters a small smile. "They are very cool."

"They don't taste of much, but obviously they're edible," I provide.

Felix takes a big bite. "What are you talking about? They taste great."

"You're easy to please," I say dryly.

"And *you* are way too humble," Felix argues. "I can't wait to try your okonomiyaki."

I flip my first 'pancake' and serve it up on a plate, covering it in sauce and mayonnaise and taking it over to Lincoln. "They sometimes put squid in them and bonito flakes on top, but I left them out today."

Lincoln gives me an appreciative look. "Thank you." I watch as he cuts a piece off and puts it in his mouth. I can usually tell if someone's just pretending to like my food or if they actually enjoy it. The pleasantly surprised expression on Lincoln's face is genuine.

"Wow. How have I never heard of this before?"

"Because you're basic," Felix jokes.

I quickly go back and make a second one for Felix. "Are you okay going vegetarian today?" I ask him.

"Sure. Why not. I wouldn't say no to anything you wanted to make but I'll be veggie in solidarity."

I finish his and take it over. He dives on it, cutting a huge chunk and shoving it in his mouth. He groans appreciatively.

"You need to open a restaurant," he says.

"Actually, I did markets for a long time but it's easier to manage my schedule around Daisy if I do the online stuff. And my supermarket deal now takes up any other spare time I might have had." I look at my watch. "Which reminds me, Daisy will be finished at school soon."

"Please do whatever you need to," Lincoln says. "We'll leave after eating."

"Oh, no. I'll ask Millicent to pick her up today. Take your time. I don't think the paparazzi will give up that easily."

"If it's not clear by 4pm," Felix says, "I'll book us a hotel."

Lincoln shakes his head. "This is all so weird."

"It does feel a bit like a spy movie, doesn't it?" Felix says. I think he's enjoying the drama a little too much.

I get out my phone and send a text to Millicent.

> Can you please pick up Daisy and bring her home? I have an important work call I can't get out of. I'll owe you big time!

I decide not to tell her about Lincoln and Felix's presence in my living room, figuring she'll find out soon enough. I hadn't filled her in on my recent communication with Felix because I knew she'd call me a stalker.

She types back.

> When you say owe, do you mean in terms of a certain car I've been bugging you about?

I know she's just continuing the earlier joke, but I'm tempted to put a big bow on Felix's car outside and trick her into thinking I'd followed through.

> Me: We'll see. I will at least return the favour and pick up Ryder for you next week.

> Millicent: Good enough. See you soon!

I can't wait to see her face when she gets here.

CHAPTER 14

LINCOLN

I hear a woman's voice before I see her.

"Holy shit, Tash! You didn't actually go out and buy me a–" She appears in the doorway and stops dead. Two kids, presumably Daisy and Ryder, comically bump into the back of her.

"Ow," Daisy squeaks. "Ryder! Why did you stop?"

"It's my mum's fault!" he protests.

Millicent's eyes go wide as she sees me. I half wave. "Hey."

Daisy peers around Millicent's legs and then stares up at Tash, looking terrified.

She quickly does the introductions. "Millicent, Daisy, Ryder, this is Felix and Lincoln."

Millicent is the first to recover and sits on an armchair next to the couch. "Hi." She then leans in, and in a loud mock-whisper says, "Blink once for yes and twice for no if Tash is holding you hostage."

Felix chuckles, and I smile faintly.

"I knew Tash's friends would be as awesome as her," Felix says.

Daisy runs over and jumps onto Tash's lap, clinging for dear life. Ryder hangs back, looking on warily.

"Lincoln and Felix are visiting us for a bit. There are some silly people trying to take photos of Lincoln at his house, so we're keeping him safe."

Daisy tilts her head to the side. "Is it the paparazzi?"

"How do you know about the paparazzi?" Tash demands.

"I remember you saying how annoying they were when you were talking to Missy about the royal family one time. You know, when you wished you could be a princess or a duchess, except you didn't like the way the paparazzi treated the women."

Tash blushes. "Ah. Thank you for that."

Millicent cracks up laughing. Felix grins, and I give Tash a look of what I hope she understands is empathy. There's nothing like children saying the wrong thing at the wrong time to make a situation awkward.

Before I can dwell on the fact that *my* children are now far away, Daisy pipes up.

"Have you been making okonomiyaki? Is there any left?"

"I can make some more if you like." Tash turns to Millicent and Ryder. "Do you want any too?"

"Yes please," they say in unison.

"One of the many perks of being friends with this one," Millicent says, jerking a thumb in Tash's direction.

"I know. Tash is great," Felix agrees. "I'm starting to wonder if I should move up to this end of the country. The people here are so hospitable."

"Yeah, but your life and career are down there," I point out.

"I guess. Although Sydney is a bit of a cultural wasteland these days. I'm probably better off moving to Melbourne. But I do have a soft spot for Brisbane."

Tash goes back over to the kitchen and starts making up more okonomiyaki mixture. Millicent joins her.

She glances over at us and presumably thinks we're too far

away to hear her talking, but I can just make out their conversation. I pretend to flick through a magazine on the coffee table but strain my ears to hear what they're saying.

"What exactly's going on here?"

"His partner left the country with his girls, and the media must have found out, so I'm letting him and Felix hide out here for a bit," she whispers.

"Seriously?"

"So don't ask anything personal."

"What about his music?"

"I guess that would be okay."

Millicent hands Tash a couple of eggs, and she cracks them into the bowl in front of her. I glance at Ryder and Daisy sitting in the corner of the room. They're staring at Felix and me.

Felix turns to Daisy. "Hey, do you have any paper and crayons?"

She looks at Tash for permission to answer.

"Sure you do. In the cupboard over there."

Daisy jumps up and retrieves them, dumping them in Felix's lap and then retreating to her spot next to Ryder.

Felix starts sketching some shapes. I can't tell from my vantage point what he's doing, but he keeps looking at me and smiling.

After a few moments, he holds up his finished drawing. It's an abstract sketch of me, and I have to say it's pretty good.

He hands it to Daisy. "I heard you like Lincoln's music."

She looks at me, embarrassed, but then snatches the drawing from Felix. "Thanks."

Tash finishes making more okonomiyaki and serves it up, giving herself some too.

The kids seem to get bored of hanging out with the adults and disappear off somewhere. The remaining four of us sit quietly. I have no idea what to say, so I continue to flick through the magazine. It's a local lifestyle publication, and one of the articles is about Tash's new supermarket deal. I'm about to comment on it when Millicent starts talking to me.

"Lincoln, tell me something that happened behind the scenes of *Sing to Me* that the public doesn't know about."

"Actually, it wasn't particularly controversial. Everyone was really encouraging. I think there's a lot more awareness about looking out for contestants' mental health these days. Not like when I was on *Have You Got What It Takes?* That was toxic. And even though the public voted for their favourite performances back then, it was mostly rigged. I didn't know this until I was being dropped from the label, but production would turn off the reverb on contestants they didn't like. That made their singing sound flat, and the public wouldn't vote for them."

Tash's mouth drops open. "So what were they implying? That they left the reverb on for you to control the outcome?"

I nod grimly. "Apparently."

"That's terrible. But also, I wouldn't believe it was the only reason you won. You *are* super talented. Remember, I've heard you sing without any microphones, and you're still amazing."

I feel the edges of my mouth turn up slightly. "Thank you."

"It's true," Felix says. "I hope you haven't been holding on to that for all those years, thinking you weren't as good as you actually are."

I don't say anything because I kind of have. It was hard not to feel like a puppet when I wasn't allowed any input into my career back then.

"I think it's difficult in all creative industries to know where you fit," Tash says. "Even with the stuff I do."

"Yeah, okay," Felix concedes. "Even though I look confident on the outside, I'm always worried everyone's going to realise I'm a total fraud one day."

"None of you are frauds," Millicent cuts in. "Honestly, I'm feeling a bit inferior myself right now, sitting in a room full of artistic geniuses."

"Says the secret government hacker," Tash teases.

Felix and I look at each other, impressed.

"Tell me how that works," Felix demands.

Millicent obliges and fills us in on the ins and outs of her job. She definitely underplays how much talent is required for such a position.

We stay for another hour before Felix stands. "I think we should go see if your house is clear. And if not, I'll go in and grab some stuff to bring to a hotel."

I stand too. "Thank you, Tash, for letting us hang out here. I really appreciate it." I step forward and give her a hug. She freezes up for a moment before returning the gesture. I don't want her to feel uncomfortable, so I let go and move on to Millicent, giving her a quick embrace as well.

Felix comes over and winks at Tash, also wrapping his arms around her. "You've been a real sweetheart. We need to talk more. Come and visit me in Sydney sometime!"

"I'll try," she promises.

We head outside and back to Felix's car.

That was a nice distraction but now I'm back in a reality I don't want to face. Paparazzi stalking me, and an empty house I'm not interested in returning to, even if I could.

What am I going to do?

CHAPTER 15

TASH

The guys leave, and I collapse on the couch. Millicent sits beside me.

"Well, that's not your everyday occurrence."

"Tell me about it."

"I must say, you did a great impression of an actual person and not a deranged groupie."

I chuckle. "Thanks." I tell her about Lincoln's daughters not being his, and she looks appalled.

"That's horrendous."

"I know! I can't begin to imagine what he's going through."

"Make sure you don't take advantage of the poor guy," she warns.

"I'd never do that!"

"You'll both end up getting hurt."

"I know. I'm quite capable of separating the fascination I have for him as a musician from being there as a friend."

She snorts. "Friend."

"If that's what Lincoln needs, it's what I'm going to give him."

"Okay. But definitely be careful."

"I will."

Ryder wanders out into the living room and complains about wanting to go home. Apparently our Nintendo Switch games aren't interesting enough and he wants to play the ones at his place.

"I suppose I should get this one home," Millicent says, nodding at her son before looking back at me. "But let me know if you befriend any other rockstars in the future. I'm still not quite sure how Lincoln ended up here, but I trust you'll behave yourself."

"I'll try."

I see them off and start the evening routine with Daisy. After she's in bed, I open Instagram. I know my obsession is bordering on unhealthy, but I can't help myself. I go to Lincoln's account to see if he's posted anything else. Not that I think he would have mentioned me or anything.

His last image is still the one about betrayal, and it has attracted dozens more comments. I ignore it and click on some older photos – the ones of him performing on *Sing to Me* and jokey selfies.

Before I can think too hard about it, I click *Follow* and then heart a few of my favourite images of him. After having him spend the day at my house, I feel like he'd appreciate the gesture for what it is: a show of emotional support.

I go to bed, glad I could help Lincoln Page in his time of need. He deserves to be happy.

❧

IT FEELS like I've only just drifted off to sleep when my phone beeps. I usually turn it to silent, but I must have forgotten tonight. I glance at the time. 3am. I wonder if someone from the other side of the world has messaged me. I often get US fans contacting me at odd hours – which of course aren't odd at all for them. I blearily look at the notifications on my screen and jolt upright.

Lincoln has followed me back. And when I click on the app, I see he's liked two of my photos. One is the teddy-bear-themed bento box I showed him on the plane, and the other is a photo of me, one of the rare ones I posted that isn't a picture of food.

I can't keep the smile off my face.

Even though he's going through the worst time of his life, Lincoln Page is thinking about me.

ON THE MORNING my bento boxes are delivered to supermarkets all over the east coast, I get a text from the head of marketing, containing pictures of my food on one of their shelves, and a feature page of their weekly magazine.

I sit there, staring at the message, realising that I've kind of made it. This is probably as good as my career is going to get. I suppose I could expand to the rest of Australia and even go international, but with everything fresh and exciting and still manageable... this is where it's at.

I forward the text to Millicent, who responds with a million celebratory emojis and a bunch of gifs featuring shirtless dancing men. I'm not sure why she thinks that's appropriate, but Millicent is always looking for a reason to post gifs of half-naked guys.

I'm supposed to be doing paperwork for the web side of my business, but it's almost impossible to concentrate. If I was in the kitchen, I'd be able to lose myself in my cooking, but the last few weeks have required me to do more of the boring administrative stuff.

I want to go to every supermarket within a fifty-mile radius and stand in the cold food section bragging to everyone who will listen that those are my meals.

But obviously I'm not going to do that. I'm a mature professional businesswoman. I will have to restrict myself to jumping around the living room on my own.

In between all the excitement, I take a moment to sit down and lose myself in the mindlessness of social media. Lincoln doesn't post a lot on Instagram anymore but I now allow myself to like each image he shares. I've decided I don't care if my followers know I'm into him. Besides, everybody seems to be into him now. His follower count has risen from thirty thousand to almost sixty thousand since the news of his split emerged.

Which makes it all the more thrilling when he notices a post I've done on my account and likes it too. He even commented on a new dish I'd made featuring characters from Studio Ghibli – one of my favourite film franchises – with an endorsement for my products. I noticed a modest rise in my own followers after that. Millicent would be happy.

A WEEK LATER, everything is starting to settle down when I see Lincoln upload a post officially advertising the dates of his multi-city tour, and it begins in Brisbane next month. I immediately buy two tickets and take a photo of them to send to Millicent.

She writes back.

> I assume you want me to be your plus-one?

> Me: Yes please.

> Millicent: OK. As long as you don't do anything embarrassing. Like throw your underwear on the stage.

> Me: That sounds like something YOU would do.

> Millicent: Ha, you're right. Well, don't let me get drunk enough to do that.

I send her the eye-roll emoji followed by a kiss.

I'm so excited to finally see Lincoln perform live. After hearing him that one time when he sang for Felix and me in Sydney, I knew that what I watched on TV wasn't manipulated.

I don't think I've been this amped for a concert in my life.

LINCOLN IS PLAYING at The Triffid, a cool music venue at the back of Newstead. It used to be an aircraft hangar in World War II but has been converted for concerts.

I haven't been to a live gig in forever. Millicent and I are actually a little late because I spent so much time fretting over my outfit. In the end I chose some distressed denim jeans, a black top with long sleeves and a cropped midriff, and some cute suede boots. Millicent has a very distinctive going-out style, sort of a gothic Barbie, so tonight she's wearing several studded belts looped around a black mini skirt, and a lacy bra top. It's the middle of winter, so she's added a Matrix-like leather coat to the look.

"Do you think we're too old for this kind of thing?" I ask.

"Too old to see a band?"

"You know what I mean. We're mums in our mid-thirties."

"Honestly, I don't think about age. There are so many kick-ass women these days in their fifties and sixties, we shouldn't be restricted by some outdated stereotype. And look at Cher! She's in her seventies and still wearing whatever the hell she wants."

"Yeah, but she's Cher."

"And you're Natasha!"

"Okay, okay. I get your point."

We hand our tickets to the security guard, and I'm quite flattered we have to show our IDs until I realise it's not to check our age, but to log our attendance.

Once inside, we make our way as close to the front as possible, which really isn't that close. The show must have sold out because the audience is tightly packed. We've missed the support act, and it seems like it'll only be moments before Lincoln appears.

Several people are on stage, tuning guitars and checking equipment. I feel the familiar buzz of energy I remember from going to big-name rock concerts as a teenager. I can't believe I'm more wired tonight than I was seeing the Red Hot Chili Peppers back in the day.

With the sound levels apparently ready to go, the stage clears, and the lights go down. The start of an old Rolling Stones song plays as Lincoln and his band take their places. The crowd goes wild, my cheering joining the cacophony of noise.

I sneak a glance at Millicent, and I'm pleased to see she doesn't look completely bored. In fact, I think she's almost as psyched as me. She just wouldn't ever admit it.

"Good evening, everyone," Lincoln says, that tingle-inducing voice booming out from the stage. "We're so happy to be starting our national tour here in my hometown and hope you enjoy what we've got for you tonight. We'll be playing a mix of covers, but also introducing a little original material."

The crowd cheers louder. I'm so pleased he's finally gathered the courage to play his own music.

He picks up a guitar and slings the strap over his shoulder. "But first, we need to get you warmed up!" He strums a loud chord, and the other guys join in for the opening of Muse's 'Supermassive Black Hole'.

I love this song, having been a fan long before *Twilight* stole it for their baseball scene. I watch mesmerised as Lincoln effortlessly emulates Matt Bellamy's falsetto. It's so sexy, seeing Lincoln up there in his element. He hasn't lost any of the appeal he had on *Sing to Me*. And while his voice sounds a bit edgier, a little angrier, I think it's an improvement. If I didn't know that he had to go through such a heartbreaking situation to get that sound, I think I'd prefer it.

We're so far back it would be unlikely for him to see us. Half of me is disappointed, but the other half would feel a little self-conscious if he knew we were here.

The show is amazing, and Lincoln's 'on', bantering with the crowd and enjoying the synergy with his bandmates.

But as with all Lincoln encounters, it's over way too quickly. He and the guys leave the stage after the last song, and I'm left wanting more.

However, apparently so does the crowd. They clap and cheer louder and louder until they return.

The first thing they play is a cover of Bon Jovi's 'Keep the Faith'. But finally, Lincoln sings the song he showed Felix and me in Sydney.

I watch, my eyes glued to him the entire time. Tonight, I imagine he's singing it for me.

And then, by chance, he looks in my direction, and the corner of his mouth turns up in a pleased acknowledgement. That one tiny gesture turns my entire body to jelly. I look at Millicent, and she gives me a knowing smile.

He finishes the song, and the band leaves for good. The lights go up, and I sigh.

"You're smitten, aren't you?" Millicent says.

"I've always been smitten."

"What do you want to do now?"

"I'm not sure. Go out into the beer garden for a drink? I'm too wound up to head straight home."

"Sounds good. I'll just go to the ladies', and then I'll see you out there. Can you order me a red wine?"

"Sure."

I head over to the bar, reliving the moment I made eye contact with Lincoln during the show.

I'm a lost cause.

CHAPTER 16

TASH

I patiently wait at the bar and order two glasses of red wine. The energy from the post-show audience is palpable. After paying for my drinks, I stand in the corner, breathing it in. These people are all feeling great because of Lincoln and his band.

Millicent takes her time but eventually finds me. She grabs her glass and rests a hand on my arm.

"Okay, I'm going to tell you something, but I want you to promise you'll behave."

I narrow my eyes at her. "What?"

"Promise?"

"I don't know what I'm promising."

"That you won't take advantage of Lincoln when we go backstage."

I jump up and down. "We're going backstage?"

She nods, obviously pleased with herself. "I had a chat with the security guard, and I convinced him to ask Lincoln if we could go say hi. He agreed."

I let out an excited squeak. "Oh my God, oh my God, oh my God!"

She hands me a pass on a lanyard to put around my neck. "You'd better get that out of your system now. We're going to act like actual human beings and not be weird around the guy."

"Have I ever embarrassed myself in his presence before?"

"I don't know. I haven't always been there. But I suspect you may have."

I think back to the plane ride where I first met him. Admittedly, I was a little frazzled at the beginning, but he clearly didn't hold it against me.

"Don't worry. You won't regret this."

"I'm actually doing this for *me*. Did you *see* the bass player?"

I laugh. "Not really. I was too busy watching the singer."

"Okay, let's go. We don't want to keep them waiting."

I feel like a giggly schoolgirl skipping out on class. We reach the backstage door and flash our passes. The guard stands aside. I've never done anything like this before.

We head down a narrow hall and come to what looks like a converted shipping container. One of the doors is open, and inside, one wall is lined with old couches. Lincoln and his band are lounging around, drinking beers and chatting.

Lincoln glances over and sees me. His face lights up in a smile very close to the type I remember from before his break-up.

"Tash! Missy! Come in!"

I nervously enter. Millicent acts like she does this all the time and struts over, plonking herself down beside the bassist.

"That was a great set," she says to him.

He's instantly entranced, but I continue to stand awkwardly near the door.

Lincoln scooches to the side of his couch. "Come, sit. I'm so glad you could make it. I would have given you both free tickets if I knew you wanted to come."

I walk over and sit beside him. I'm just as nervous as I was back on the plane. "Don't be silly. We were happy to be paying customers. That show was amazing. And you did your own stuff!"

"Yeah. The guys and I decided it was time. And Max, the guy who signed us up for this whole thing, was happy for us to experiment. I think it went down okay."

"It went down phenomenally! I was in the middle of the crowd, and I know for a fact they loved it."

He smiles appreciatively. "I'm glad you think so. Hey, are you right for a drink?"

I hold up my half-full red wine. "Good for now."

He downs the rest of his beer and slams the bottle on the coffee table in front of him. "I think I need something a little stronger than this." He turns to his drummer. "Beau, where's the tequila?"

Beau's sitting beside a box and pulls a bottle out, handing it to Lincoln.

"Now we need shot glasses." He looks around. "Does anyone know where the shot glasses are?"

A passing crew member stops. "I can get some from the bar."

"Good man. Thank you."

Lincoln focuses on me. "How's your business going?"

I find it unsettling to be on the receiving end of such an intense gaze. "Great, actually. We almost ran out of stock in the first few days, but we managed to speed up production in time. Initial feedback is that everyone's loving the product. Hopefully next year we can expand the range and number of outlets that stock them."

He suddenly reaches out and touches my hair. "I love your fire hair."

Oh. My. God.

"Thank you."

It would be so easy to flirt back and run my hands through his curls but I know I have to tread carefully. It hasn't been that long since Rachel and the girls left. He'd still be mourning their loss.

Possibly even starting a court case to regain some sort of visitation rights. I don't need to complicate his life.

He sits there, continuing to look at me with a small smile. I don't know what to do, so I stare at the floor.

"Do I make you nervous?" he asks.

"A little."

"Why?"

Because you are hot as hell, and I've been dreaming about kissing you for quite some time.

"I don't know. You just do."

He chuckles. "I–"

He's cut off by the crew member returning with a bunch of shot glasses. He plants them in Lincoln's hands.

Lincoln lines them all up on the table. "Who's having shots?"

Millicent looks over. "Me."

Almost everyone in the room yells some form of agreement, so Lincoln fills them all. He hands one to me and picks one up for himself. He holds it up in the air. "To a successful tour."

The rest of the band cheers. I raise my glass in Lincoln's direction and then slam it back.

I wince as it warms the back of my throat.

Lincoln's already pouring himself another.

And then another.

He doesn't stop until he's had six shots of tequila in less than two minutes.

He leans back on the couch and puts his arm out so it's resting just behind my head.

I could never in a million years have imagined being in this situation but I'm still wary. Even more now that Lincoln's had all that alcohol.

"How's Daisy?" he asks.

"She's good. With her grandparents tonight."

"So you don't have to be home by any particular time?"

"Uh…"

His eyes twinkle. "Relax. I'm just making conversation."

"I *do* have a work call in the morning, but it's not something I need to prepare for."

He nods, satisfied.

"Was your first show everything you hoped?" I ask, trying to get back on safer ground.

"Definitely. I'm really looking forward to the rest of the tour."

"Where are you going next?"

"Next weekend, we head south down the east coast and then to all the other states after that. We're playing four nights a week until almost the middle of October."

"That's exciting. I'll bet you'll get lots of groupies fighting over you."

Why did I say that? That makes me sound like a jealous girlfriend.

He raises an eyebrow. "I guess we'll have to wait and see. We didn't get many the last few years when we were doing smaller gigs." His face clouds over. "But then I never really hung around after a show, because I always wanted to get home to the girls."

"I'm sorry. I shouldn't have said anything…"

"No, it's okay. I knew I'd have to deal with these feelings eventually. This is my first show without anyone to go home to."

It takes all my resolve not to offer my bed tonight. But that wouldn't help anyone.

I look at Millicent. She's rubbing her hand up and down the bassist's thigh.

Lincoln follows my gaze and laughs.

"It looks like she's enjoying herself."

"I apologise for Millicent. She's not a shrinking violet by any means."

"You don't have to apologise for your friend. We're all grown adults here letting off steam."

He leans his head on my shoulder, and I tense.

He talks softly. "You know, I thought the worst thing that

could ever happen was when the record label dropped me a year after I was on *Have You Got What It Takes?* But you don't realise that everyone loves a comeback. Unless you're a complete tool, people like to see you rise again and be happy. But with Rachel…"

"It's hard to come back from, huh?" I say quietly.

"I don't know *how* to come back from it. How do you get your head around the fact that someone you loved actively lied to you for four years?"

"I'm not sure. I guess just give yourself time to feel all those crappy emotions and surround yourself with good people."

"But I thought *she* was good people! I never once suspected she was anything but genuine."

"I'm so sorry you're going through this. I know, to a lesser extent, what it feels like to be abandoned."

"How did you cope after your ex left?"

I smile dryly. "I didn't really. I just knew I had to be strong for Daisy and get on with it. My parents and Millicent have been amazing. If it helps, I promise to always be real with you and try to be what Millicent has been to me."

He leans his head closer to my face. "You're awesome, Tash…"

I feel like things are getting a little out of control. Lincoln's drunk and vulnerable, and if I let this go any further, we're both going to regret the aftermath.

I gently extricate myself from him and stand. "I should go. But please contact me anytime if you need to vent."

He smiles ruefully. "Sure."

I go over and grab Millicent's arm. "We have to go," I whisper in her ear.

She looks up, grimacing. "You're killing me, Tash."

"Sorry, but I need to give Lincoln some space. If you want to stay, I'll catch an Uber on my own and see you later."

She sighs loudly. "No, no. I'll go with you."

She finds a pen in her handbag and writes her phone number

on the bassist's arm with a big love heart. "Call me," she says before following me back outside.

"I can't believe *you're* the one making *me* go home," Millicent says.

"It would have gotten messy if I'd stayed."

She stops and looks at me with respect. "I'm so proud of you right now."

"Thanks. It was pretty hard saying no to the guy, but it was the right thing to do."

Now, if only my raging hormones would agree with me.

I think I need a long cold shower.

CHAPTER 17

LINCOLN

I never drink like this. What's wrong with me? I'm just like my parents, getting hammered because I'm too scared to face unpleasant emotions. I should be better than that.

As soon as Tash and Millicent leave, I come to my senses. I didn't even think about how poor Tash must have been feeling. She doesn't deserve someone who is so mentally fucked up. The woman is sweet and caring and beautiful. But any feelings I have for her are confused. I still love Rachel, despite everything she did to me. And if she suddenly returned with the girls and begged my forgiveness, there's a big chance I'd take her up on it.

But would I, really? Should I? Trust is kind of a big deal with me, and it's been well and truly betrayed with Rachel keeping such a monumental secret from me. For four *fucking* years! Who *does* that?

It's been two months since I've heard from her or the girls, and it's killing me. I've contacted a lawyer to try to figure out what to do, but everything's moving so slowly. I've called Rachel's parents in the UK – since Rachel disconnected her mobile from Australia – but they wouldn't tell me anything the first time I spoke to them, and now they won't even answer the phone.

I've contemplated flying over there and forcing them to let me see the girls, but I'm contractually obliged to remain in the country until the tour is over. Even before today, I had to stay for rehearsals. I tried to explain to Max what happened, but while he was sympathetic, he wouldn't let me leave.

For now, I'm doing everything I possibly can to get access.

It's so damn hard though. The least Rachel could do is let me video call them. Surely they would have asked about me. What would she have told them? Every day I wake up and struggle to get out of bed, wondering where they are and what they're doing. I still can't process that they're not biologically mine, but I don't even care. I wonder if their real father knows. Has Rachel reconciled with him? Are they all now one big happy family in London? I hate that I don't know anything.

And on top of that, everything in our house reminds me of them. I'm kind of looking forward to getting away and staying in hotels for a while so I can pretend they're all still waiting for me at home.

Man, I'm messed up. And I resent that Rachel timed her departure so it would essentially ruin the experience of my first proper tour. But at least I'm staying occupied.

I look at my watch. Almost 2am. I'm going home to sleep.

I throw my stuff in the back of a cab and say goodbye to the guys. I hear them talking about continuing the party back at one of their houses, but I'm not interested in joining them.

By the time I get home and take my equipment inside, it's almost three. But now the last thing I feel like doing is sleeping. I open my laptop and scan social media. Rachel's blocked me from all her accounts, so I can't look at any photos of the girls she might be posting.

I mindlessly scroll through Instagram, looking at the latest offerings. And then I see a picture Tash published yesterday. It's a photo of her meals stocked in a supermarket with her standing beside them, pointing and grinning.

I instantly click the heart icon and stare at her face for a moment. Something stirs in me that I didn't think was possible. A tiny, tiny shred of hope that I might one day be happy again. And if I could end up with someone as talented and beautiful as Tash, I'd be very lucky.

I still feel bad about how I treated her tonight, so I google online florists that can deliver at short notice.

After selecting a bouquet and paying a ridiculous amount in delivery to ensure it gets to her house this morning, I turn off my computer, feeling a bit better.

The sun is just peeking over the horizon by the time I finally collapse into bed.

The combination of having done a big show and drinking more than I'm used to, along with the emotional toll of the last few months, finally hits me. I close my eyes and black out, welcoming oblivion.

CHAPTER 18

TASH

One downside of having a young child is that even when she stays with my parents overnight, I still wake up early the next day. Millicent decided to go back to her place to sleep last night, and I'm wide awake at 6am, despite not getting to bed until around two.

I'm not hungover, because I didn't drink that much, but I have that slightly weird floaty feeling you get after a big night out and not much sleep.

I make myself a strong coffee and sit on the couch, enjoying not having anything to do. I told Mum and Dad I'd collect Daisy at ten, so that's four hours alone to contemplate the events of last night.

Part of me wishes I'd let Lincoln kiss me. I could have just taken it for what it was, a guy who was hurting and needing a bit of love. But I knew we'd both regret it today. I don't think I could separate my emotions, and I would be left wanting more.

But then I feel like I might have been doing him a favour, performing the rebound role to help him get over Rachel. It was kind of selfish of me to deny him that chance. Plus, at least if he'd chosen me, he wouldn't have had to worry about some other less suitable woman taking advantage of him.

Except what makes me more suitable than anyone else?

My reverie is interrupted by a knock at the door. I don't usually get anyone coming over this early.

When I answer, I see a delivery guy standing there, holding a large bunch of colourful gerberas. No one ever buys me flowers! And to have them delivered at 7am on a Saturday morning would not be cheap.

I take the bouquet and sign for them, not opening the card until I'm in the kitchen.

I'm so sorry about last night. Please forgive me.
Lincoln.

My heart feels like it's going to burst. How did he organise these at such short notice? A sad thought occurs to me, and I wonder if he still wakes up super early too, as a residual side effect of living with the twins for three years.

What's more likely is that he continued partying and hadn't yet gone to bed when he ordered them.

I think about his behaviour last night. Lincoln was drunk and a bit morose, but he was never disrespectful. There was no reason he should feel bad enough to send me apology flowers.

As I don't have his phone number, I write him a direct message via Instagram, thanking him for the gift.

He doesn't reply, so I run myself a bath and enjoy the last bit of quiet I'll have for a while.

My daughter will be home soon.

DAISY and I have a chilled-out day together. I half-nap while she colours pictures of Disney characters in one of her activity books and watches cartoons on TV.

At 6pm, there's a knock at the door. I assume it's Millicent since she often drops by on weekend evenings, and I'm thinking she'd want to debrief about last night.

But it's not her.

It's Lincoln.

His hair's all tangled like when I met him on the plane. And his scruff is a little wild, but it makes him look sexier than ever.

He gives me a sheepish smile when I open the door.

"Hey."

"Hey! How are you today?"

He rubs his temples. "A little under the weather, but it was my fault. I just wanted to check you got my flowers?"

"I did. And I messaged you on Instagram to thank you. I don't have your mobile."

"Ah. I've been avoiding social media the last few days."

I belatedly realise I haven't invited him in. "Do you want to come in? Daisy and I are just hanging out."

"If that's okay with you? I'm not interrupting mother-daughter time or anything?"

"Um, no. You do realise my daughter is a bigger fan of your music than I am? And that's saying something."

He chuckles. "In that case..."

I usher him in. I'm glad I wasn't doing anything embarrassing like scrolling through his photos on my laptop. Or playing his music.

Daisy looks up when he enters the living room, and her eyes widen.

"Hi, Daisy," he says, the way only a guy who has experience with kids would greet a child. "It's great to see you again."

"Hi."

He points to the flowers, which are in a vase on the hall table. "Did you know these are gerbera daisies? Just like your name?"

She smiles. "Really?"

"Yep. I chose them specially."

My bones start to liquefy. If only this guy didn't have so much emotional baggage to process, I'd be putting Daisy to bed and throwing myself at him.

"Are you hungry?" I ask. "I can make something."

"No, no. I mean, I'm hungry, but I don't want you to cook. How about we order in? What's your favourite food, Daisy?"

"Pad Thai," she answers immediately.

He laughs. "In that case, I think we should get some Thai food delivered." He pulls out his phone. "Do you have a preferred place around here?"

"Try Phon's."

"Do you like curry?"

"I'm easy," I say, and then blush when he raises an eyebrow and gives me an amused smile.

"Yes, a green curry would be great," I add hurriedly.

He types into his phone and holds the receiver to his ear. Daisy and I watch, probably with equally smitten expressions as he places the order.

I busy myself by pouring some iced water and carrying it over to the coffee table.

"Can we watch *Frozen*, Mum?" Daisy asks.

"Oh, I'm not sure Lincoln will want to watch that," I say.

Lincoln hangs up the phone. "What was that? Did I hear someone say *Frozen*?"

"Yes! Mum says you wouldn't want to watch it."

"Of course I want to watch it! Do you know I can sing all the words to 'Let It Go'?"

I can imagine this situation must be incredibly difficult for him. I'm sure the only reason he knows that song is because of his girls.

"I know all the words too!" Daisy says, as if it's the best coincidence in the world.

"Then we'll have to sing together."

I press my hands to my chest. I don't think my heart can take any more of this adorable exchange. I revisit the idea that perhaps I fell asleep weeks ago before my flight to Sydney and never woke up. It's possible I'm in a coma.

We sit down in front of the TV, and I set up the movie.

Daisy plonks herself on a beanbag on the floor, leaving the couch for Lincoln and me.

I awkwardly rearrange the cushions so we have a couple each to lean on. The armrests are a little worn, and I feel a bit self-conscious about not having a more stylish house to present to him. I know he potentially doesn't have a lot of money of his own but I still wish I had some fancy furnishings.

The movie begins and I try to relax. But who can act naturally while watching *Frozen* with their daughter and a freaking rockstar sitting next to them?

I try to sit as still as possible, so I don't accidentally bump him. But then my mouth gets all dry, and I reach down to get a sip of water, and in the process, my arm brushes his. He jumps back in much the same way I did on the plane that time.

I look at him incredulously, and when our eyes meet, I see he's nervous. *Lincoln Page* is nervous around *me*!

The realisation makes me giggle softly.

"What?" he asks.

"Nothing, sorry. I guess I find this all a bit random, having you here in my living room watching a Disney movie."

He grins. "I guess that *is* a little strange."

"But it's great," I hurriedly assure him. "I'm really glad you're here."

"Me too. It's nice to do something normal."

I'm almost afraid to ask, for fear of setting him off, but I'm curious.

"Are you still at your place in Ashgrove?"

He nods. "But probably not for much longer. I'm thinking I'll put it on the market and rent somewhere smaller for a while until I figure out my next move. I'm not sure if Rachel will ask for money for the girls, but I want to have some set aside just in case."

"But she deceived you!" I protest.

"I know. It might not matter though. The courts can be unforgiving with that kind of thing. There was a big case where a guy ended up losing a dispute against his ex in the same situation as me, and he had to pay all the expenses, including his ex's."

"That's horrible."

"I know. In my mind, the girls are still mine, so I'm putting aside my frustration and focusing on what's best for them. If they need money, I'll give it to them."

"You should still fight for visitation rights."

"Believe me, I'm working on it."

The food arrives, thankfully lightening the mood a little.

We pause the movie to serve up, and then watch a bit more of Elsa and Anna's sisterly love.

When 'Let It Go' comes on, Lincoln keeps his promise and sings it word for word with Daisy. She's too shy to join in much, but I can tell it's made her night. However, the act seems to take its toll on Lincoln, and I can see a wave of emotion cross his face as he sings the chorus.

When it's over, he abruptly stands. "I have to go."

"Oh, okay. Of course. I'll see you out."

"No, no. I'll be fine. Thanks for your hospitality. It's been great."

He hurries out, leaving me wondering if he's all right.

I send him a quick message on Instagram, thanking him for coming over, and I give him my phone number for any future communication.

A few minutes later, my phone dings with a text.

Thank you for tonight. You're awesome.

The message ends with a daisy emoji.

I rejoin Daisy in the living room, saving the number from the text to Lincoln's name, and beaming a large smile.

Even though the circumstances aren't ideal, I am so glad the guy's in my life.

CHAPTER 19

LINCOLN

I don't know what made me drive over to Tash's house and invite myself to stay for dinner but I'm glad I did. It was the most normal I'd felt in weeks. Tash has such a sweet and understanding nature, I can't help but be drawn in.

And the more I spend time with her, the more I like her. She manages to make single parenting look easy. And Daisy is the most adorable child outside of my own girls. I really enjoyed their company.

I had to leave quickly at the end of the movie because I was worried I would say or do something stupid. I have so many weird emotions running through my brain and no way to process them.

How can I want to kiss Tash when I still love Rachel? Would Tash just be a rebound? I was with Rachel for so long that I don't know what would normally happen next. What's the right amount of time to take before moving on? If I asked Tash out in the near future, would I be sabotaging a chance for something real between us later?

And then there's the question of whether Tash even has feelings for me. She turned me down last night, and rightly so, but was it only because I'd been drinking? She's a successful and confident woman. What would she want with an ex-reality-TV contestant who just had his family abandon him?

I wander around my empty house, and the silence illustrates how depressing my life is right now. It feels wrong not to have the girls asleep in their bedroom and Rachel curled up on the couch nearby.

As soon as this tour is over, I'm flying to the UK. I don't care if I have to spend all my money on travel and a private detective. I'd do anything to see the girls again.

I kick off my shoes, get myself a beer out of the fridge, and flop down in front of the TV. I hate sleeping in my bed alone and have been crashing on the couch instead. Late-night infomercials have been keeping me company.

Jeez. My life's pathetic.

I HAVE five days before the tour continues, and I am *not* looking forward to them. Five days to dwell on the absence of my children and the continued feelings of betrayal from Rachel.

While I don't need the money, I ask my friend Eli if I can do a few extra shifts at his coffee shop. As it turns out, one of his regular employees is sick, so he takes me up on the offer. It's a little boutique place on Elizabeth Street, and for some reason, no one seems to notice who I am when I'm there. Not that it bothers me if people judge. Just because I was on TV and perform in the entertainment industry doesn't make me any more special than people who work in hospitality. In fact, hospitality is harder. The pay should be better.

I spend Monday and Tuesday lost in the mindlessness of making coffee and wiping down tables. In between, I work on some new tunes. My lyrics aren't literal, but they definitely help me process some of the emotions I'm going through. Betrayal.

Despair at not seeing the twins. And hope after spending time with Tash and Daisy.

On Wednesday, I get home from the café and find a cooler bag on my doorstep. Upon opening it, I find a bunch of Japanese meals. I take them inside and read the note stuck to one of the containers.

I thought you might want to try a few of my favourite dishes :)
Tash
P.S. They're all vegetarian friendly.

I pull out each container, labelled with their contents. The first one is a bento box with teriyaki tofu, tempura vegetables and a salad doused in sesame dressing. The next is okonomiyaki, which I remember from the day Tash cooked for me. The third is a cold soba noodle salad, and the fourth is some nori rolls. They all look delicious, and I have to stop myself from opening all of them and eating everything right there and then. Instead, I leave out the bento box and put the rest in the fridge.

As I eat the tofu, I find myself comparing Rachel to Tash. Rachel would never have left food on anyone's doorstep. Somehow, I know this isn't the first time Tash has done it.

My shattered heart doesn't ache so much today. And in fact, a tiny part of it is now reserved for Tash. A warm and happy corner I hope will continue to expand.

I send her a text.

Thank you for the food. I'm already eating the bento box, and it is amazing. XOXO

She writes back.

> I'm glad you like it. I knew you'd probably be busy with rehearsals, so I thought you might not have time to cook properly.

While I'm not too busy to cook, I *have* been feeling sorry for myself. Making dinner for just one person has not seemed worth it.

> Me: I really appreciate it. We'll have to hang out again sometime soon. I'll let you know when I'm back from the tour.

> Tash: Sounds good. Keep me posted!

I stare at my phone, smiling. I love how natural everything feels with that woman. I'll have to keep in touch with her while I'm away. The middle of October is too long to wait before I talk to her again.

⁊♪

I'M ABOUT to collapse onto the couch for the night when my phone rings. Felix.

"Hey! How are you?" I ask. He's been texting most days to see how I am, but this is the first time he's called in a while.

"Good. Looking forward to seeing you again when you come to Sydney."

"Me too. It's annoying because this is the first time I can crash at your place without worrying about anything getting damaged, but Max is making me stay at a hotel with the band."

"How come?"

"I don't know. Something to do with wanting us to be easily accessible. We have a radio interview before the show, so I'm just doing what I'm told."

"That's fine. As long as I'm on your VIP list for tickets?"

"Of course. I've reserved a seat for you in the front row."

"Can I bring a plus-one?"

"Sure. Who are you thinking?"

"Tash."

I'm caught off-guard. "Oh, right. I keep forgetting you two are friends without me."

He laughs. "You sound jealous, buddy."

"No, no. Have you already mentioned the idea to her?"

"Nope. I thought I'd leave that up to you."

If I'm being honest, the idea of inviting Tash to one of my other shows is exciting. But I'm not sure if it's a good idea. What if she rejects me? What if she thinks the gesture is too over the top? Offering someone a ticket to an interstate concert is kind of a big deal.

"But then I'd have to consider the airfare…"

"We'll split the cost if you're worried about money."

"It's not that. It's just, don't you think it will scare her off?"

"Um, you think a hot rockstar offering free flights and concert tickets to someone will *scare* them?"

"It could."

"I think the real question is, does it scare *you*?"

"A little."

"And why's that?"

"Because I'm fucked up, Felix! I haven't heard from Rachel or the girls in months! I can barely stand it."

"Yet you sent flowers to Tash and spent the evening with her and her daughter."

"She told you that, huh?"

"We're practically besties. Of course she told me."

"Did she also tell you that I tried to kiss her, and she turned me down?"

"Ah, yes. Because you were drunk."

"But that might have just been an excuse." I don't want to tell him about the food she dropped by. He'd just use that as extra ammunition against me.

"It wasn't. Believe me."

"Did she tell you specifically?"

I can hear the smile in Felix's voice. "She didn't have to. It was obvious by the way she said it."

"I don't know… I don't want to rush things…"

"All right, well, let me put it this way. How would you feel if Tash was dating someone else?"

"I…" Actually, the idea makes me feel a little weird. And in a very surprising realisation, when I think of Rachel with someone else, I don't feel nearly as conflicted.

Felix interprets my silence as a victory. "See?"

"Okay. I'm not promising anything, but I'll think about it."

"Excellent. Tash would be good for you. You need someone grounded like her."

"You know what? Maybe I do."

"I knew you'd come around eventually. Go call her now!"

"Uh, no. It's almost 10pm. I'll wait until a decent hour."

"Rockstars don't wait until 'decent hours'."

I shake my head. "Goodbye, Felix. I'll see you soon."

I hang up and look into space. The guy has a point. Tash is definitely someone I need in my life.

I'll just have to make sure I don't do anything stupid and mess it up.

CHAPTER 20

TASH

*I*t's been just under two weeks since I last saw Lincoln when I get another delivery. This time, it's not flowers, but an envelope.

Upon opening it, I find several things:

1. A ticket to Lincoln's Sydney show tomorrow night.
2. An airline ticket for tomorrow to Sydney.
3. A handwritten message:

Tash, please come to Sydney. I've already talked to Millicent, and she's lined up to look after Daisy. Felix says you can stay in his spare room. He wants to see you!
(So do I.)
Lincoln.

I laugh out loud. If I had any singing talent myself, I'd be feeling like Lady Gaga in *A Star Is Born*. This kind of thing doesn't happen to me. And I can't believe Millicent didn't tip me off. I call her immediately.

"I thought *I* was the one you were supposed to be loyal to!" I tease.

"Ah. You got the tickets."

"Yes! And you didn't warn me!"

"Lincoln wanted it to be a surprise."

"I'm not sure I should go."

"Then don't."

"What do you think I should do?"

"Whatever the hell you want. You're a grown woman."

"But what if he wants to... you know..."

She cackles. "You mean, what if he wants to screw your brains out? Isn't that what you've wanted for forever?"

"I... I don't know. Maybe. But what if I'm just a groupie to him?"

"He doesn't need to fly a groupie down to Sydney. I'm sure he could find plenty of women after the show if he only wanted a one-nighter."

"So you think he's serious?"

"I'm not a mind-reader. You'll need to ask him that yourself."

"I don't want to get hurt, Missy."

"I know, hon. But sometimes you have to just go with the flow. See what happens."

"Okay. And you're sure you'll be fine to look after Daisy?"

"Of course. I've got a hot date next week so I'll need you to reciprocate."

"Definitely. Who's the date?"

"His name is Constantinos. He's recently moved to Australia from Greece."

"Oh, I hope it goes well."

"Me too."

We talk a bit longer about our week, and then I hang up. I text Lincoln.

> Thank you for the tickets. I'd love to see your show. But don't get any ideas!

I send it before I have a chance to change my mind. He writes back straight away.

> What ideas might they be?

He posts a winking emoji beside it.

> Me: You know exactly what I mean. Anyway, I'll see you tomorrow. Can you give me Felix's address?

> Lincoln: He'll pick you up from the airport. All you have to do is get on the plane.

> Me: You've got it all worked out, haven't you?

> Lincoln: It's my way of apologising properly for my behaviour after the show in Brisbane.

> Me: You have nothing to apologise for. But thank you. I'm looking forward to it.

Tomorrow suddenly seems both too soon and too far away.

But regardless, I'm cautiously excited to see where this might lead.

❧

FOR THE ENTIRE flight to Sydney, I'm all jittery. Anyone looking at me would think I'm scared of flying, but it's quite the opposite. I love travelling. I'm not sure what the plan is once I land, so I'm already dressed appropriately in case we go straight out, in a form-fitting knee-length black skirt and a sparkly top. I even begged my hairdresser to touch up my colour at late notice, and she used a special dye that will produce an extra-cool effect tonight.

Once I land, I spot Felix right away. He's pretty tall and by far the best-dressed guy waiting outside the arrival gate. Plus, he's holding a little chauffeur sign with my name on it.

He sees me immediately too. "Tash, you look gorgeous as always." He gives me a hug and insists on taking my bag out to his car, where it's waiting in some fancy valet parking zone.

Apparently Felix owns a similar Audi to the rental in Brisbane, only this one is black. We begin the drive over to Manly where he lives.

"Do you want to be a complete tourist and drive across the Harbour Bridge? Or are you happy to take the tunnel?"

"I'm fine with the tunnel. I assume it's a little quicker?"

"About ten minutes."

"Then yes, let's do that."

"Have you visited Sydney often in the past?"

"Not really. Maybe a handful of times in total, including when I met you. And I haven't been to Manly since I was a teenager."

"It hasn't changed a lot. At least, I don't think it has."

"You're lucky to live near one of the country's most famous beaches."

Felix nods, concentrating on driving. "I know."

"Have you spoken to Lincoln today?"

"Yes. He was hoping he'd be able to get away before the show but the band's doing some media thing beforehand, and then they have a soundcheck."

"Ah."

"So I was thinking we'd have a few drinks at my place, and either eat in or grab something on the way to the show, and then Uber over to the venue. They're playing at the Enmore Theatre."

"That's a pretty well-known place, huh?"

"It is. I think they're expecting over a thousand people tonight."

"That's awesome. It was very kind of Lincoln to invite me."

"He never stops talking about you, so I told him if he wanted you in his life, he needed to start making an effort."

Warmth flows throughout my body. "That's sweet and all, but I'm sure he's still got a lot to process after what happened with Rachel."

"Yes, but if he dwells on the past, it will take him a lot longer to move on. Besides, I never liked Rachel. I couldn't tell Link that because she had him wrapped around her little finger, but I always knew there was something shady about her. Now I know I was right."

"She looked nice enough on the show."

"Of course she did. She was always preening for the camera and playing the devoted partner and mother. But in real life, she was nothing like that. I didn't get to see them much, because I was living here and they were up there, but from the stories I heard, she was all about image. Don't tell Link you know this, but he told me she was disappointed he didn't win *Sing to Me* and only got a national tour of mid-sized venues as a result. It wouldn't bring in as much money as a recording deal and an international stadium tour."

"But he's only just getting restarted! It's unrealistic to expect he'd go from nothing to everything overnight."

"Exactly. I need him to move on so that when he does achieve all of that – which we both know he will – she doesn't suddenly change her mind and worm her way back into his life."

"So you see me as a stepping stone in his recovery?" I ask lightly.

"No, of course not. I think you're beautiful, strong and independent, and I can see you as a great team. Who says you need a whole bunch of rebounds before you settle back down?"

"I'm sure the odds of settling down with someone who's

recently experienced a messy break-up are against you more than if they've been single for a while."

"I don't know. He seems like the kind of guy who likes to be settled, and you'd be perfect for him."

I don't say anything else. If that's true, I'll have to think about whether *I'm* ready to settle down.

What do *I* want?

Actually, I think I'm getting waaayyy ahead of myself. We've only hung out as friends a few times, unless you count his one drunken attempt at hitting on me. Which I don't.

We arrive at a lovely modern three-storey house, and Felix pulls into the driveway. He takes me inside and up to the third level, where he puts my bag in the guest room. The entire place is open plan, with lots of glass looking out onto the bay and all the sailboats below.

"Wow. I can see why you'd hesitate to relocate to Brisbane."

"This house is pretty special. Link thought it would be a bit presumptuous to invite you to his hotel, so I was happy to offer you my place."

"Why isn't he staying here?"

"He and the band are all booked together as part of the tour. But I'm just going to put it out there now; please don't feel guilty if you don't end up wanting to take advantage of my hospitality."

I blush. "Felix!"

"Honey, we're all adults here. You do what you want."

"Okay, thank you. I think I need a drink after that."

He laughs. "Let me give you a quick tour of the rest of the house, and then I'll show you where I keep the hard liquor."

Felix shows me his room, with tasteful timber panelling behind the bed and the kind of swishy double-layer curtains you see in fancy hotels. The spare rooms are just as nicely furnished, with white linen and fluffy pillows on all the beds. Every level has an amazing view of the water, and I understand from the expensive-looking vases and bowls adorning every surface why Felix wouldn't want young children staying here.

Back downstairs, he pours us champagne, and we sit out on a terrace overlooking the pool. I feel like I'm in one of those R & B film clips where they have a bunch of women twerking in bikinis.

My life is pretty surreal right now.

CHAPTER 21

LINCOLN

I'm super nervous about tonight. Not only because it's my first big show in Sydney, but also because I'm wondering if it was the right move inviting Tash down here. Am I rushing it by organising such a grand gesture? I do like her, but I'm not sure what I want from her, or what she expects from me. We barely even know each other. But what I *do* know is that she is bringing light into my life at a time when I very much need it. And it doesn't hurt that she's incredibly attractive.

I guess I'll have to go with the flow and see what happens. It's not like I invited her to share my bed tonight or anything. I just wanted to see her. And also, with her and Felix being friends, it makes sense they're hanging out too.

In the afternoon, a limo picks me and the guys up to take us to one of many pre-show interviews Max booked for the tour. I did a few of these during the filming of *Sing to Me,* but this is the first one I'm doing with my band. It's exciting and feels more real. The station's asked us all to come along to play a song, but I'll be the only one speaking during the interview.

I sit down on one side of the studio desk while the guys start setting up their instruments at the back. The DJs, Axel and

Amber, are well known for their witty banter, and this radio segment usually gets good ratings.

Axel starts talking. "Lincoln Page, it's great to have you and your band here ahead of tonight's show at the Enmore Theatre. We've heard positive things about the tour so far. How are you feeling about it all?"

"Yeah, we're really enjoying the experience. It's great to be out touring the country and playing for everyone again."

"We've been told you're starting to incorporate a few originals into your setlist. Tell us about that."

"I think the guys and I realised we had more to offer than just covers, and fortunately the audiences have been very kind so far. We're excited to see where it all leads."

"Should we be looking for any hidden meaning in the songs? You did go through a rather messy break-up recently…"

Damn it. This is not the direction I wanted this interview to go.

"Uh, I guess you'll have to listen to the songs and decide that for yourself. But I'm not one for airing my grievances through music."

Axel laughs. "Very diplomatic answer there."

Amber cuts in. "Leave him alone, Axe." She then looks at me. "But I can't imagine being single again has hurt ticket sales with a certain demographic. Have you found you're seeing more female fans at your gigs?"

Jeez. I hope Tash isn't listening to this. I laugh nervously. "I'm not sure. I don't keep track of who's in the audience."

"So modest. Maybe there's already another lucky lady in your life?"

Shit. I really, really hope Tash isn't listening to this.

"You'll just have to wait and see," I say mysteriously.

Amber chuckles. "Interpret that how you like, listeners."

Axel grins at me. "All right. Now it's time for a little *This or That*. Do you know how the game works, Lincoln?"

"Yes. Even my daughters know how to play."

"Good. Let's get straight into it then. Cookies or ice cream?"

"Ice cream."

"Pop music or rock music?"

"Rock."

"Coffee or wine?"

"Coffee."

"Summer or winter?"

"Summer. Definitely."

"Blonde or brunette?"

"Can I say hair that looks like fire?"

"Um, that's oddly specific, but okay. *Frozen* or *Moana*?"

I think of the night I spent with Tash and Daisy and smile.

"*Frozen*."

"And the last one… Japanese or Mexican food?"

"Japanese," I answer without hesitation.

"There you have it, folks. Lincoln Page is a sushi guy." Axel smiles blandly at me. "While we've got you and the band here, will you play us something? We did a poll with our listeners, and they unanimously requested your final performance from *Sing to Me*. Will you do the honour of playing 'Never Tear Us Apart'?"

"Sure." Even though the question sounded spontaneous, we'd been told of this in advance, so we came prepared.

"All right. Take it away, guys."

I join the boys at the back of the studio. As I grip the microphone, I clear my mind to focus on the music. That's all that matters right now.

AFTER THE INTERVIEW, we head back to the hotel to get ready. I have to admit, I'm enjoying the whole rockstar-in-a-limo thing, even if it's only for a short while.

As we cruise through the streets of Sydney, I get out my phone to see if I missed any calls while I was at the station.

My heart stops when I see one from an international number. The country code is from the UK.

There's no message on my voicemail, so I press *redial*, holding my breath.

No one answers. Shit. Was that Rachel?

I do a reverse phone number search, but nothing shows up online. I save the number under Rachel's name with a question mark. What if she finally wanted to talk but I was too busy doing press for my show?

But also, what if something's wrong? The girls might be hurt… someone could have been in an accident…

And then I catch myself. If something was seriously wrong, she would have left a message. And I don't even know if it *was* her.

I hate that I have no idea what's happening. The tour still has six weeks left, so I'm stuck until then.

We pull up at our hotel, which happens to be the Shangri-La again. This time I have mixed emotions. During my last visit, Tash was an acquaintance, and I was still living in blissful ignorance with my partner and children.

But now…

We check in. Max has booked two rooms, so I have to share with one of the guys. I would much rather be hanging out at Felix's, but I don't want to look like I'm not a team player.

Beau and I have been friends the longest, so we take one room, and Jesse and Andy take the other. We agree to meet back down in the lobby a couple of hours before the show.

I try calling the UK number again, and this time someone answers.

"Rachel?"

"Hi, Lincoln," she says neutrally.

"Oh my God! It *is* you. I'm so glad you finally got in touch. How are the girls?"

"They're fine. They love London. There's so much more to do than in Brisbane."

"Can I talk to them?"

"No, I dropped them off at pre-school a few minutes ago."

"What about when they get home? Can you call me then?"

She sighs. "I wish everyone would move on. Between you and the bloody girls whinging to speak to each other…"

"What do you expect? As far as we all knew, they were my daughters, and I was their dad. And in my mind, that's still the case. Just because of your fuck-up, you shouldn't keep punishing everyone forever."

"Jesus, Lincoln. I've never heard you sound so aggressive. I wish you'd had some balls like that when we were together. I might have stuck around."

I almost choke on my tongue. "Are you kidding me?"

"Lighten up, all right? It's not like you're living some closed-off hermit life or anything. I still read the news."

"I'm on tour, Rachel. I tried to pull out but I would have been sued if I did. Either way, you can't possibly think I'm happy with the way things are."

"I really don't care how you feel."

Holy shit. Has she always been this cold? I take a deep breath. There's no use me yelling at her. "Then why did you call me?"

"Ah, I didn't. The girls had my phone in the car on the way to pre-school, and one of them must have accidentally selected your number."

"Rachel, please. Let me talk to the girls sometime. I don't care what time of day it is, or for how long. I only want to hear their voices and know they're okay."

"Fine. I'll think about it."

"Thank you. I really appreciate that."

"Make sure you remember how generous I'm being when my lawyer gets in touch."

"I will." My heart sinks, wondering whether she's going to try to take everything from me. But I can't worry about that now. I'm just glad she's considering letting me talk to the girls.

"I have to go," she says abruptly before hanging up.

I stare at the phone, not sure how to feel.

But then it beeps, and a message comes through.

Can't wait to see the show tonight!

Tash.

A sense of calm washes over me. I'm seeing Tash soon. Beautiful, sweet Tash.

I'm going to play this next show for her.

Because we both deserve to be happy.

CHAPTER 22

TASH

*I*n the end, Felix and I decide to stay in and eat, so Felix orders some Vietnamese rice paper rolls and bao buns to be delivered.

Just after 9pm, we catch an Uber over to the Enmore Theatre. Our names are on a special list, so we're waved through and led down into a VIP area at the front. I definitely feel like Lady Gaga.

When the venue's spotlights go down, a row of UV lighting takes over, and Felix whoops in delight.

"Tash! I love your hair! Lincoln won't be able to miss you."

I smile. That's what I'd been hoping for. The hairdresser used a special dye that makes my hair glow under a black light. I hadn't been completely sure if the venue would be set up accordingly, but I knew it would be worth it if it was.

A driving beat revs the crowd. I cheer as loudly as everyone else. Maybe louder.

The band members take their positions, and Lincoln follows them out, strutting over to the microphone stand.

He glances in our direction, and his face lights up in a delighted smile. He winks before focusing on the opening song.

I'm entranced the entire show, not even aware of Felix beside me. It's like I'm in one of those cheesy movie scenes, where it's just Lincoln and me in the room. And it's not like he's even watching me exclusively. Although I have to admit, every time his eyes wander in my direction, my belly tingles.

His final song is 'Sunshine of Your Love' by Cream, and his gaze lingers on me for at least half of it.

The crowd roars with approval when the final notes fade, and the guys don't keep everyone waiting long before they come out for the encore.

Once they've disappeared again, a security guard approaches us.

"Will you two come with me, please?" he asks. "I have orders from Mr Page to take you backstage."

Felix laughs. "Orders from Mr Page, huh? It's nice to be famous."

We follow the guard out the back to an area bigger than at The Triffid. And this time, I feel the energy buzzing between Lincoln and me immediately. When he sees me, he grabs my hand, dragging me away from everyone else. I glance back at Felix, and he grins, clearly not worried about being abandoned.

"Where are we going?" I ask Lincoln.

"Here." He shoves open a door to a small dressing room and pulls me through. After kicking it closed behind us, he pushes me against the wall, leaning forward and finding my lips with his.

Oh. My. God.

It's almost too much for my brain to comprehend. The sensory overload from the show, and now kissing this guy after wanting him for so long almost makes me black out. But I sink into the moment, finally getting a chance to run my hands through his hair and breathing him in. His mouth is warm and soft, and I want to rip his clothes off on the spot.

I've dreamt about this moment for months. Come to think of it, the fantasy probably started fourteen years ago – although I never thought it would come true. And somehow, the reality is even better than what I conjured in my head. The feeling of his lips, and his hands brushing the sides of my face as he keeps my mouth on his. Lincoln seems to have absorbed all the energy from the crowd, and it's now swirling between us... adrenaline, power, sex.

Eventually, we come up for air.

"Wow," I say, smoothing down my shirt.

He laughs. "Yeah. Sorry. I couldn't help myself. You looked so damn gorgeous tonight. I'm surprised I could remember all the words to my songs."

"Ha-ha – really?"

"There's something about you, Tash. I can't get you out of my head. And I know it's not ideal, considering all the crap I have going on, but I'm so happy you agreed to come see the show tonight."

"Me too."

He looks at the door. "I suppose we should go back to Felix. I feel bad for leaving him."

"Yeah." I sneak in one last kiss and stroke his cheek. "You're amazing."

He smiles happily. "I'm glad you think so."

We head back out to the main backstage area and find Felix drinking red wine with the band.

"That was quick," he jokes when he sees us.

"Buddy! Be cool, hey?" Lincoln says in a faux-stern voice.

"Sorry. God, you two are so hot together."

I blush, revelling in every moment. If only Lincoln didn't have all that recent baggage, I would be on cloud nine. As it is, I'm still on cloud eight. Eight point five even.

Beau hands us a beer each, and we join them. I sit and watch while Lincoln breaks down the night's show with his bandmates. In between, Felix and I chat about our work.

Around midnight, Felix looks at his watch. "Are we going to

move this party back to my place? There's plenty of room for everyone to crash if you don't want to go all the way back to the hotel afterwards."

Lincoln raises an eyebrow at me as if to ask whether I'm okay with that.

"Whatever you guys want to do is fine," I say.

"Then let's go. We have our limo waiting out the back."

I almost laugh out loud. "A limo?"

"Yeah, I know. It's a bit cliché, but I think Max wanted us to play the part."

We head down a side alley where a proper black stretch is waiting for us. Lincoln opens the door for me. I slide in, not sure whether to feel like as much of a cliché as the limo or not.

There's champagne inside, and Felix immediately opens it. He seems right at home in this kind of environment. But then I suppose being an in-demand artist would occasionally provide you with experiences like this.

Lincoln sits next to me and whispers in my ear. "Are you okay? This isn't freaking you out?"

"I'm good. Thanks."

Felix hands me a glass of bubbly and pours one for himself before passing the bottle around. The other guys forgo glasses and drink straight from the bottle. When it gets to Lincoln, he waves it away. "No, I'm all right for now."

I make a mental note of his refusal. I've no idea if he's had anything else other than the one beer, but I wonder if he's trying to show me that there's not going to be a repeat of what happened after Brisbane.

Back at the house, Felix pumps up some Massive Attack on his expensive sound system and sets us all up with more drinks. Lincoln agrees to have another beer but refuses anything stronger.

Felix smiles at me. "How are you coping, being the only female here?"

"I didn't notice until just now, but I think I'll manage." I wink.

The other members of the band all go outside to smoke. Whether it's weed or cigarettes, I have no idea, but neither of them appeal to me. I stay with Felix and Lincoln inside.

Felix turns to me. "Okay, Tash, since you and I are now practically besties, I think we need to share more of our personal histories. Tell me how you lost your virginity."

I snort. "You don't mess around, do you?"

"Nope. But if you need a moment to gather your thoughts, I'll go first." He doesn't wait for me to reply before continuing. "So I was sixteen, and everyone already knew I was gay. Thank God my parents were cool and the people at school who counted were supportive. Anyway, it was the end of the year, and we'd all just finished exams, so we went down to the beach to let loose. It wasn't far from here actually."

He smiles wistfully. "Someone suggested Spin the Bottle, and everyone decided we had to play by strict rules, so guys could kiss guys and girls could kiss girls. And then Spencer Lockheart, the hottest guy in school, spun the bottle and got me. I was expecting him to back out or just give me a kiss on the cheek, but oh my God, it was the hottest thing ever. It turned out Spencer was gay too, but still in the closet. Until that night. Needless to say, things progressed very quickly."

"Aw, that's sweet," I say. "Were you together for a while?"

"For about a year afterwards. And then his parents decided to move to France, and it wasn't practical for Spencer to stay behind. We tried to stay in touch, but it was hard. And then he met some fancy French guy and forgot about me."

"Still, at least your first was someone you really cared about."

"Yours wasn't?" he asks.

I suddenly feel self-conscious, knowing Lincoln is listening. I glance at him, and he looks at me thoughtfully.

Ah, what the hell. "Not exactly. I was seventeen, and I liked this guy who worked at a nearby café. He was older than me and so cool. I basically went broke buying coffee there every day for six months until I worked up the courage to ask him out."

"The guy was stupid if he didn't realise you were interested before that."

"I think he *did* know, but he just wasn't fussed either way. But for some reason, that made me want him more. Like I had to earn his affection." I blush at this admission. I don't usually tell this story, and I certainly would never tell it in front of a guy I was trying to impress.

Felix nods. "We've all been there."

"He agreed to meet me at a restaurant that night since I was too young to get into a bar or nightclub. And then he proceeded to get drunk before dragging me to his car so we could do it in the back seat. He finished. I didn't. So maybe it only half counts."

Felix laughs. "Again, we've all been there."

I let out a puff of air. "I went for the bad guys for way too long."

I check Lincoln's reaction. He gives me a small supportive smile.

"I think I need a little more alcohol in my system before I share my story." He looks at the red wine in Felix's hand and goes to take it, but Felix won't let go. He tries again, but the wine splashes out of the glass and all over Lincoln's shirt.

Felix gives him a pointed look. "That's what you get for trying to steal my wine. You're lucky you didn't spill it all over the carpet."

"Sorry. Lesson learned."

Felix points upstairs. "You can use my shower. And raid my clothes for something to wear after."

"Thanks, buddy." Lincoln stands and heads for the stairs. "I need a shower anyway. That theatre was hot tonight."

I watch him leave and wonder if the whole incident was just an excuse for him to get out of talking about how he lost his virginity. It didn't sound like he was particularly happy about it.

"Tash, are you comfortable?" Felix asks. "Do you need to get changed too?"

"Oh, I'm fine," I say.

"Damn, you were supposed to say yes, so I could ask you to bring me down a shirt as well." He pulls at the collar of the obviously man-made fibre.

"All you had to do was say 'Tash, I'm lazy, can you get me a shirt from upstairs?'" I tease.

"Tash, I'm lazy, can you get me a shirt from upstairs?" he parrots. "Please?"

I laugh. "Sure. Any preferences?"

"Just something breathable. Maybe a white cotton T-shirt."

It isn't until I'm halfway up the stairs that I realise Felix is almost certainly playing matchmaker. I inwardly groan. I'm so clueless.

I reach the top of the stairs just as Lincoln comes out of Felix's room holding a shirt and pants. Before he can say anything, I talk first. "Felix sent me to get him a shirt."

Lincoln nods, as if I've been given a gravely important task. "You can do that. But first..." He takes my hand and pulls me towards the bathroom. He fixes me with a gaze so intense I think I might melt into a puddle on the floor. "Would you like to join me?"

I don't trust myself to speak, so I overtake him and lead him into the bathroom.

He closes the door behind us and slowly pulls my shirt over my head, kissing my neck before unclasping my bra and dropping it to the floor. I pull his wine-soaked shirt off and run my hands across his smooth chest.

He steps away for a second to get the water in the shower running.

As steam fills the room, he dims the light and comes back over, planting kisses on my mouth, my earlobes, and my collarbone. He kneels down and unzips my skirt, sliding it over my legs and looking into my eyes the entire time.

Holy moly.

This *cannot* be real.

CHAPTER 23

LINCOLN

J wake in the morning in Felix's spare room, with Tash still sleeping beside me. I watch her breathing peacefully, and I feel content. Last night was exactly what I needed – an evening with a woman who I genuinely like as a person.

I have no idea what happens from here, but I'm not under any delusions that we're ready to jump into a serious relationship, complete with children involved.

Also, I have to consider what Tash wants. She might decide that last night was enough for her. And we still don't know a whole lot about each other. What if we have nothing in common? And even if we do, we're both building careers. That would mean limited time for us to spend together. And that's not even taking into consideration any legal issues I'll need to resolve with Rachel and the girls.

Reality is complicated.

Tash opens her eyes and smiles. "Hey."

"Hey, yourself."

She sits up and combs her fingers through her hair. That amazing flame-coloured hair. "How are you feeling?"

"Good. Better than I've been in a long time actually."

She smiles as she traces circles on my chest with one of her fingers. "I'm glad to hear it." She's thoughtful for a moment. "Hey, last night you were hesitant to talk about how you lost your virginity."

"Uh, right. Yeah. I guess because the person I lost it to betrayed me so deeply."

She frowns. "You don't mean…"

I nod grimly. "Rachel was my first."

I know what Tash is going to ask next, so I beat her to it. "No, you're not the second. Rachel and I were on and off before the twins came along, and I wasn't exactly a saint in the off times. But if I'm being honest, this is the first time I haven't thought about how me sleeping with someone will affect my relationship with her." I look deeply into Tash's eyes. "Thank you."

She pulls me into a gentle hug. "No, thank *you*."

We sit there, holding each other for a few minutes. I've never felt so calm.

Eventually, she loosens her grasp. "I might grab a coffee. Do you want one?"

"In a minute." I pull her close and start kissing her again. Her skin feels ridiculously soft. I'm just making my way down her body, kissing as I go, when my phone buzzes.

I groan.

"You should probably get that," Tash says.

"Ignore it," I say, continuing onto her thighs.

It stops ringing, but then starts again.

"You can answer it." She stands and finds a black slip in her bag that she slides over her body before sneaking out of the room to give me some privacy.

"Hello?"

"Hi, Lincoln, it's Carter."

Carter is my lawyer. I told him to call me anytime he had news about Rachel or the girls.

"Oh, hey. What's up?"

"I've finally heard from Rachel's lawyer. She wants half the house."

I figure this is what she was talking about when she said to remember how generous she was being. "Okay. What else?"

"You know we can go for paternity fraud?"

"I do but I'd rather not drag this out for any longer than we have to. And after the High Court overturned that other case..."

"That was a long time ago. But at least you won't have to pay child support. With Rachel admitting she had a DNA test done, she gave up any rights to financial compensation."

I rub my face tiredly. "Look, just tell her I'll put the house on the market after I've finished my tour, and I won't sue for paternity fraud, but she has to be reasonable. I want to be able to see the girls, so if that means providing money for some of their expenses, I'll deal with it."

"Are you sure? We can ask for visitation rights without paying for them."

"Please just find the easiest and quickest way to resolve it all."

"Okay. Sorry to bother you on the weekend. I'll be in touch next week."

"Thanks, Carter. I'm on the road until around the tenth of October, but I'm usually available during the day."

"No problem."

I hang up and go to the kitchen, trying to keep my mood upbeat.

"Everything okay?" Tash asks.

"Uh, I just have some stuff to sort out when I'm back in Brisbane."

"Anything we can do to help?" Felix asks.

"Nah. But thanks."

Felix pours me a coffee. I take it, lost in thought. A legal conversation about my ex was the last thing I felt like this morning.

Felix heads off to shower, leaving me alone with Tash. I've no idea where the other guys have gone.

Tash takes a deep breath. "Hey, I want to say, I don't expect anything from you because of what happened last night."

I give her a measured look. "Okaaayyy…"

"It's only… I don't know. I'm not sure what you want, and with our careers and everything else…"

"Are you breaking up with me?" I ask lightly.

"No! Of course not!" She pauses. "I didn't even realise…"

I laugh. "Relax. I don't have any expectations about you or this." I point my fingers between the two of us. "I know I really like you, but I'm also pretty messed up, and I don't want to inadvertently cause you any pain."

"I can handle myself. But I have Daisy to consider… and work. I need to make sure they don't suffer in any way."

"I totally understand. Can we let the situation unfold naturally?"

"That's fine with me."

I go over to where she's sitting on a barstool and tilt her chin up to meet my face before kissing her softly. "Thank you for being awesome."

She swallows. "*You're* awesome."

CHAPTER 24

TASH

*L*incoln's heading to Canberra later in the day, and he has another press thing to do before he leaves, so Felix drives me back to the airport at lunchtime. When I said goodbye to Lincoln, I told him I'd leave it up to him to dictate the level of contact we had from this point on. He still has a big chunk of his tour left, so we'd be limited to chatting on the phone or online until sometime in October.

I get home and immerse myself back into life with Daisy and my expanding empire. It's quite a feat, juggling the school routine, my online business, and ensuring the supermarket roll-out continues to go smoothly, so the only time I really get to think about my love life is when I'm alone at night in bed.

Lincoln sends a couple of quick text messages over the following week, mostly thanking me again for going to Sydney and saying he's looking forward to when we can next catch up.

And then from the second week on, I don't hear anything at all. I stalk his Instagram for clues of what might be happening, but he only posts images from the tour and information regarding the band.

I message Felix to see how he's doing, but also to indirectly ask whether he's heard from Lincoln, but I don't get any insight there either.

It's quite disappointing, but a tiny part of me always sort of expected this to happen. I should be grateful I got to be part of Lincoln's world for the time I was.

And then two things happen in very quick succession.

It's six whole weeks since I was with Lincoln in Sydney when he texts me late one night.

> We just finished our last show on the tour, and I'd like to see you when I get home. Is that OK?

I write back.

> Sure. Call me when you're settled in.

The next day, it occurs to me that my period's late.

And a trip to the pharmacy confirms it.

I'm pregnant.

CHAPTER 25

LINCOLN

The tour passes in a blur. Each day we're either flying or driving to a new town, or rehearsing. We don't usually play live Monday to Wednesday but a lot of the downtime gets eaten up with travelling. Very occasionally I get to wander around the city we're in, but mostly I try to catch up on sleep or talk to Carter about the latest developments with Rachel.

In the week after Sydney, I text Tash a few times to see how she's doing. I loved our night together, and I could quite possibly see us exploring something when I'm home. But then in the week after that, Carter sends through an email that shatters me, leaving no room for thoughts of new relationships.

Rachel has suddenly decided she wants the whole house but still refuses to let me see the girls. The only concession she'll make is a video chat once a month, and an in-person visit once a year, for ONE weekend in the UK, that will be supervised by an agreed-upon intermediary.

I can't believe she thinks that's being generous. I should have listened to Carter at the beginning and gone for paternity fraud. The money doesn't bother me, so I could almost deal with giving her the house if she allowed me real access to the girls, but to only give me two damn days out of a whole year is not acceptable. I immediately call Carter.

"I thought we'd agreed on half the house and a meaningful amount of time with the girls."

"Yeah, well, I guess she thinks since you're trying to avoid court, it gives her more leverage to get what she wants."

"I can't do this, Carter." I stare bleakly out the window. I'm in a small town in Western Australia, on our way to Perth. I wish I could enjoy the experience more and what has so far been one of the highlights of my career. But Rachel seems intent on destroying everything good in my life.

"We can still sue. Although, she did mention that your name isn't on the girls' birth certificates, so that might make things more difficult."

How did I not know I wasn't on their birth certificates? I think back to when we had to send away the paperwork and vaguely recall her telling me she'd taken care of it. I suppose I never thought to look at it once it arrived in the mail.

I'm so angry, I can barely get the next words out.

"Tell her she can have half the house, and I want to bring the girls back to Australia four times a year for two weeks each trip. And I'm allowed to visit them in the UK whenever I'm there. I don't *want* to go to court but tell her I won't hesitate if she's not reasonable."

"Okay. I'll keep you posted. I'm sorry, Lincoln. I see this stuff all the time, but it still sucks to watch my clients go through it."

"Thanks, dude. I'll wait to hear from you."

After hanging up, I check the time. The guys will be wanting to have dinner soon.

I start composing a text to Tash, telling her I'm thinking about her, but that I need a bit of time to sort my life out before getting in touch again. I hope she understands. It's not fair on her if I don't have the emotional availability she deserves.

Beau enters our hotel room. "Link, buddy. We're starving. You coming to eat with us?"

I shove my phone in my pocket and stand up. "Of course."

I follow him out to the elevator. The call with Carter plays over and over in my head.

I hope he manages to convince Rachel's lawyer that my suggestion is fair. The idea of a court case makes me feel sick, but I'll do it if it means I have a better chance of seeing Isabella and Madison properly again.

AS THE WEEKS WEAR ON, I'm grateful the tour allows the guys and me a chance to bond more. We were always good friends but being forced to spend an extended period of time together has really given us an insight into each other's lives. I don't want to bring them down by telling them what Rachel is putting me through, so when we talk about women, I occasionally mention Tash. I take their good-natured ribbing in the spirit it's intended.

"Dude, you should have taken some time off before jumping into another relationship. Enjoy the backstage benefits on tour."

"It's not much of a relationship right now, but I hope that it will be at some point. Which means I'm not going to jeopardise that." I don't tell them I probably wouldn't indulge, no matter the situation. I'm just not a casual hookup kind of guy.

But either way, throughout the tour, I've hung back after a few shows, and I know for a fact the guys aren't participating in mass orgies either. I think the most I've seen is Jesse making out with one girl in Hobart. I know the guys like the idea of the sex, drugs and rock 'n' roll lifestyle, but they're not living it. And life on the road isn't like the image portrayed in the movies anyway.

It's actually quite an exhausting and inconvenient process. While we're lucky enough to be paid for the gigs and have our accommodation and travel covered, Max hasn't exactly been throwing money at us. We travel in a cramped van most of the time and fly economy when we have to cross large spaces quickly. I've learned to switch off from the world with my noise-cancelling headphones and my favourite true crime podcast on the longer journeys.

The shows have been everything I could possibly hope for though. The crowds have been amazing everywhere, and they've responded well to our setlist – which we slightly changed over the tour to include a few more originals. The guys and I have talked about planning a full album once we get back to Brisbane, and after that, we'll talk to Max and see if he's interested in helping us sign with a label.

Our final show was tonight in western New South Wales. The guys are all in one of the other hotel rooms celebrating, but I chose to come back to my room and chill out for a bit.

I've barely heard from Carter, apart from a few generic emails saying he's still working on a deal. I've managed to compartmentalise my feelings in order to stay sane. If I dwell too much on the fact that I might only get two days a year with my girls, I will lose it completely.

I open Instagram and flick through my feed, stopping at Tash's account. She's posted a new bento box, one with a Nintendo Mario theme. I can't believe how talented that woman is. I click the heart beside the image. And then I realise I'll be home tomorrow, and I can finally see her again. That is, if she wants to see me. She never replied to my last message, which I have to admit is a little worrying, but I hope it just means she understood the situation.

I open up my texts and am about to compose a new message when I see that I never finished typing the previous one. Holy crap. I know even if it had gone through, it wouldn't have been an ideal situation, but it would have been better than nothing. Tash must think I completely abandoned her for the whole tour!

I type quickly, telling her I'd like to see her when I get home. I want to apologise and explain everything now, but I think it would be best if I did it in person. It's only a two-and-a-half-hour drive back to Brisbane tomorrow, so I'll head straight to her place.

I've realised I need her in my life, regardless of what happens with Rachel and the twins.

Because I think we're a really good match, and I want to make Tash feel as happy as she makes me.

CHAPTER 26

TASH

*S*hit. I don't know how this happened. Lincoln and I were really careful, and admittedly, things got a little out of control in the shower that night, but we didn't actually have sex until we were in the bedroom afterwards… and he was wearing a condom.

It must have broken somehow. It had been so long since I'd slept with anyone, I might not have realised anything was wrong. That whole night's a blur. I'd had a few drinks, but I wasn't completely drunk. I one hundred per cent remember seeing the condom.

Oh God. What am I going to do? I'm a single mother with an expanding business. And how will Lincoln react? He's barely coping with his existing family drama. How's he going to handle *this* news?

I figure I'll have a couple of days before I have to deal with him, since he'll be coming home today, and I told him to only call me once he's settled.

I'll need that time to process this. Except I'm not sure any amount of time will help.

I text Millicent and tell her I need her to come over. The kids are at school, and thankfully my bestie works from home.

I can be there in an hour. Is that all right?

I text back in the affirmative.

I pace around the house, my heart pounding, and then I freak myself out, wondering if my stress is harming the baby. I take a few deep breaths until I finally feel my pulse slow.

In what feels like no time at all, there's a knock at the door. I look at my watch. It's only been twenty minutes. I guess Millicent was able to get away sooner. I wonder if she's psychic and somehow knew it was important to be here immediately.

"You know me too..." I trail off as I open the door.

Lincoln's standing there.

I almost swallow my tongue. "Uh, hey!"

"Were you expecting someone else?" he asks, eyes twinkling.

"Oh, just Millicent. She said she was going to drop by. Wow! I didn't think I'd see you so soon."

"I got straight in my car as soon as we arrived in Brisbane. I haven't even been home yet. But I've been a terrible communicator..."

"You have," I agree. Then wonder if I really should be doing the guilt trip thing considering the news I'm about to drop on the guy.

"I want to apologise. I actually started writing you a message back when I was in WA but I forgot to send it. Can I come in so we can talk?"

"Sure."

He leans in and hugs me. I hug him back and wonder if he can already tell there's something different about me. But of course he wouldn't know. *I* wouldn't even know except for that stupid little plastic stick with the blue line.

He stands back for a moment and looks at me. Under any

other circumstances I would shiver, because that expression is one of someone I know cares about me, despite the radio silence.

I lead him into the living room.

"Did you want anything to drink? Or eat?" I offer.

"No, that's fine. Actually, maybe some water if that's okay?"

"That's definitely okay." I pour us both glasses and take them over to the couch.

"How was the tour?"

"It was good. Sold out nearly every show. We're now hoping Max will represent us permanently and help us score a recording deal."

"Oh! That sounds exciting. If you almost sold out, I'm sure he'll be interested."

"Exactly."

I study Lincoln's face. He doesn't look as happy as he should. "But?" I prompt.

"Oh, the music stuff is fine. More than fine. It's just everything else. I owe you a huge explanation. I'm not usually the kind of guy who sleeps with someone and then never speaks to them again."

"I didn't think you were. And I told you upfront I was happy to go by your schedule. I knew you had the tour and other stuff to deal with."

"It's true the tour was all-consuming, but that's not the reason I wanted space. I just didn't want to drag you into the mess I was in with Rachel."

I'm trying to find the right moment to explain my news to Lincoln, but he keeps talking. I figure a few extra minutes won't make a difference. And I'm worried about his reaction. This might be the last time we have a friendly conversation.

"Is everything sorted out with her now?"

"Not exactly, but I hope to hear something from my lawyer soon. Either way, I'll be selling my house, so I'll organise that over the next few weeks. The main thing I'm trying to work out is how to see the girls again. Rachel is being a *little* difficult in that regard."

"Oh. Does that mean you might have to relocate to the UK?" My heart stops, waiting for the answer.

"No, no, nothing like that. But I *will* probably go over at some point. The only problem is, Rachel registered the twins' birth certificates without my name down as the father, so I'm going to have limited rights moving forward."

My mouth drops open. "She left you off the birth certificates?" I know I did the same to Daisy's dad, but that was because he made it very clear he didn't want to be a part of her life. I would never do that to someone I was in a serious relationship with.

"Yeah. It's all a big mess."

Crap. I can't drop my news on him now, can I?

"Anyway, I needed to tell you that I want you in my life, but it might be a little messy. I'm not sure if that's something you're willing to commit to, and I'll totally understand if you'd rather not." He'd been looking down at the floor while talking but gazes up at me from behind those curls while waiting for my response. A small trace of a hopeful smile plays on his lips.

I let out a deep breath.

"You think things are messy *now*..."

He narrows his eyes.

"I... uh... I'm actually pregnant."

His eyes widen. "What?"

"I'm not sure what happened, but I'm guessing something went wrong that night we were in Sydney..."

"The baby's mine?" he asks, stunned.

"Yes! I haven't slept with anyone else. I haven't slept with *anyone* other than you since Daisy's dad!"

Lincoln looks like he's going into shock. And while I'm trying to be the strong, sensible one here, it's pretty damn hard, especially considering what happened the last time I announced to someone I was pregnant.

There's a knock at the door. It takes a second for me to remember I'd invited Millicent over. I look at Lincoln apologetically and go to let her in.

"Okay, what's going on? Your message was vague but urgent."

I tilt my head towards the living room. "I'm just talking to Lincoln."

"And you needed me, why?"

I suppose now is as good a time as any to tell her.

"I'm pregnant," I whisper.

"Holy shit!" she yells.

I slap her arm. "Shh…"

She points manically at the living room. "And Lincoln's the dad?" she mouths.

I nod.

"Do you want me to come back later?"

"I don't know…"

"Millicent, you can come in," Lincoln calls out.

Millicent shrugs and walks towards the living room. She's never been one to shy away from a difficult situation. Even one that doesn't concern her.

"So… you knocked up my bestie, huh?"

He lets out a puff of air. "Apparently."

"What do you mean *apparently*?" she demands, getting upset on my behalf.

"I don't mean anything by it," he says tiredly. "I only learned the news myself five seconds ago."

"Listen, buddy. Just because some little bitch lied to you once before doesn't mean Tash would do it too. She's the most honest person I've ever met, and you'd be damn lucky to have her to co-parent this baby. For the record, Daisy's a dream child, and it's solely down to her. So you better get your head around the situation and support her."

"Hey, Missy, give the guy a break. He's dealing with a lot of other stuff at the moment. This is kind of the last news he needs right now."

Lincoln looks at me. "I hate to ask this, but are you really sure it's mine?"

"I'm going to punch you in the face if you ask that again," Millicent warns.

"Yes, it's yours. I'll even get a paternity test to prove it," I say.

"How soon can you do that?"

"Really? You're going to insist on the test because of some selfish cow in your past?" Millicent spits.

"Missy, that's not really helping. I think I need to talk to Lincoln alone. I didn't know he was coming over when I invited you around before. Maybe I can go to your place later?"

She gives Lincoln the stink-eye. "If you even so much as think of making my friend cry, I *will* kill you."

He smiles weakly at Millicent. "You're a good friend, Missy. I'll do my best, but I agree with Tash. We need to sort this out, just the two of us."

"Okay." She does the I've-got-my-eye-on-you gesture to Lincoln and then the call-me-later fingers to me. I nod and watch her leave.

When it's just the two of us, I sigh. "I'm so sorry, Lincoln. I don't know what to do."

"It's okay. We'll figure it out. And I know it's uncool to keep bringing it up, but I really couldn't handle it if this baby wasn't mine."

I make a decision.

"You know what? I appreciate where you're coming from, but even once you know it's yours, I don't expect anything from you." I get out my phone and type into Google. "I can get a paternity test done in about four weeks, so I'll book it so you know for sure. I have nothing to hide. And in the meantime, maybe we both need some space to come to terms with it."

He looks at me, and I can see tears in his eyes. He comes over and wraps his arms around me. "You want space?"

"It's probably for the best."

I'm only saying that because I don't want to look clingy – and I want him to want me on his terms. I don't tell him that having him reject me after already being rejected by Daisy's father would absolutely ruin me. It wouldn't serve any purpose other than to make him even more upset.

But I don't know how I'd feel if he completely shut me out until he got the results of the paternity test. It would mean he never really trusted me, and then I'm not sure I could have him in my life after that.

He kisses my forehead and stands.

"Okay. I'll go. But I'm not abandoning you."

I swallow a lump in my throat.

We'll see.

I DON'T REALLY FEEL like talking to anyone after Lincoln leaves, but Millicent texts me and orders me to go to her place.

There are still a few hours before I have to pick up Daisy, and I know I won't be able to concentrate on work today, so I drive over to her apartment in Bardon.

She hands me what looks like an elaborate cocktail when I walk in the door.

"Missy, you know I can't drink right n–"

"It's a mocktail," she says cutting me off. "I'm not silly."

I gratefully take it from her, and we sit on her couch in the living room. I point to a glass on her coffee table that looks like it contains the same drink. "Does that one have alcohol in it?"

"No. I'm not a big fan of day drinking. It makes me sleepy."

I smile, despite the cyclone of emotions competing for

attention in my brain. "So if it didn't make you sleepy, you'd be permanently drunk?"

"Maybe. Although work does frown upon being hammered while I'm hacking into secret government accounts. And I do have a son I have to pick up from school later. But enough about me, we have to talk about you!"

"I don't even know what to say."

"How did you manage to get pregnant? Didn't you only sleep with Lincoln the one time?"

"Yep."

"And you decided to skip birth control?"

"No! We used a condom. But obviously it failed."

"Obviously. How did it go with Lincoln after I left?"

"I asked him to give me some space."

"Is that what you wanted?"

"Not really. But I didn't want him to feel trapped. He has to decide on his own if he wants to be part of this."

She shakes her head. "While I sort of get that logic, I think you need to tell him how you really feel." She takes a sip of her drink. "Man, who would have thought when you were watching *Sing to Me* back in April that you'd now be carrying the child of one of its contestants?"

"Oh God. This is surreal. I can't be pregnant with Lincoln Page's baby!"

"Forget about the fact that he's a rockstar for a second and tell me how you feel about Lincoln, the person."

"I really, really like him, Missy."

"Do you love him?"

"I don't know. Until recently, this was all a fantasy. I don't know him well enough yet."

"I guess the only way to figure it out is to actually spend some time with the guy."

"But I just sent him away!"

"I understand why you did, but I'm not sure it will make things any easier."

"I guess I'll give him a couple of weeks to make the first move. And if he waits until after I get the paternity test results, I'll know my answer."

She gives me a troubled look. "I hope that doesn't happen. But either way, I'm here for you, babe. As are your parents."

"We'll have to wait and see about my parents. I haven't told them yet. I can't imagine what they'd think if I ended up being a single mother with two children to different fathers. You know my mum is kind of old-school."

"She still loves you so I know she'll help. But if you need moral support when you go visit, I'll come with you."

I give her a tight hug. "Thanks, hon. I don't know what I'd do without you."

"Right back 'atcha. I'm actually surprised *you're* the one with the unexpected pregnancy. I always thought it would be me."

"There's still time," I joke.

"Easy there, babe. One new little creature in our lives is going to keep us very busy for a while. Besides, I've only had a few dates with Constantinos. He might not appreciate me talking about us having babies just yet."

"Oh, crap! I've been so wrapped up in my own stuff, I forgot to ask how it's going with him!"

She smiles goofily. "Actually, he's really sweet. I'll introduce you guys soon."

"I'm so glad you've found someone nice!"

"Me too. So maybe we both finally struck it lucky."

I gaze out the window. I hope that's true and Lincoln turns out to be the guy I thought he was.

And if not, am I strong enough to do this all over again on my own?

I guess I might not have a choice.

CHAPTER 27

LINCOLN

*B*loody hell. Tash is *pregnant*? And *I'm* the father? How did that even happen? I wasn't drunk that night in Sydney, and I remember using a condom. I know they're not one hundred per cent infallible, but still.

I leave Tash's house in shock. What I thought was going to be a slow and hopeful reunion turned into a nuclear explosion.

As I drive home, I think about our conversation. She wants space. And she made it clear I wasn't needed in her life. But did she mean it? Or was she just saying it because she didn't want to impact my already-complicated situation?

One thing is for sure. I am not abandoning that woman. But I have to sort out something with the twins. I call Carter.

"Hey, I'm back from my tour, so I can start organising the house sale. Any news from Rachel?"

"I'm afraid not. Her lawyer is stalling."

"Why?"

"I don't know. Probably hoping you'll just give up."

"I'm never going to give up. Is there anything you can do to speed things along?"

"I'm trying. But with Rachel out of the country, her lawyer is using the difficulties of communicating in different time zones as an excuse to drag things out."

"Please see if you can get some sort of resolution in writing in the next few weeks."

"Will do."

I hang up, frustrated. That's it. There's no more time for messing around. If I'm about to have another child, I need to make sure I can also still see my first two.

And if Rachel and her lawyer are using the time difference as an excuse, I'm going to call their bluff and fly to the UK.

I book a flight to leave tomorrow and return before the end of the week. I don't want to be away from Tash for too long, especially considering she thought I abandoned her before. It's going to be exhausting, but I did just spend two months on the road. What's another few days?

I would endure anything to see my girls again.

Since Tash told me she wanted space, I figure I'll contact her next week. Hopefully, that's enough time. Because I can't be away from her for longer than that.

AFTER A RIDICULOUS AMOUNT of time in the air, and a brief stop in Singapore, I finally reach Heathrow at around lunchtime London time. It's the opposite part of the day in Brisbane, which is really going to mess with my body clock. I didn't sleep much on the plane, but the idea that I might be about to see my girls again keeps me going.

I've only visited Rachel's parents once, and that was on the trip when the twins were conceived with another man. As my Uber pulls up to the front of their house, my stomach churns. It's almost more than I can take.

I nervously walk up the driveway and stand at the front door. After a few deep breaths to calm my nerves, I knock.

No one answers. I can hear a TV playing loudly inside so I knock a bit harder.

Finally, I make out the sound of footsteps walking down a hall, and the door opens.

It's Rachel's mum, Hazel. She stands there, staring at me for a moment. "What do you want?"

"Are the girls here?" I ask.

"Nope."

I'm not sure what Rachel told Hazel, but she's not acting as if I'm blameless here.

"Can you tell me where they are?"

"Why do you want to know? From what I've heard, you haven't been a good provider for quite some time."

Ah. So that's the angle Rachel's playing. I wonder if she told her mother anything else.

"I'm sorry she felt that way but I did the best I could. I haven't seen my daughters in several months, and I would be really grateful if you could tell me where they are."

She doesn't say anything, continuing to look me up and down. Eventually she sighs. "Rachel rented a place in Notting Hill. I'll just go get the address."

"Thank you."

I stand on the doorstep while Hazel takes her time.

When she returns, she hands me a slip of paper with the details on it. She looks conflicted for a moment before seeming to decide something. "Rachel's my daughter, so my loyalty is to her, but I respect any man who flies halfway around the world to see a couple of girls who aren't his own."

I smile gratefully. "They'll always be mine, regardless of their DNA."

She looks out at the street. "Do you have a rental car?"

"No. I was just going to call an Uber."

She picks up a keychain hanging from a hook in the hall.

"Take my car. I don't need it today. But I'd appreciate it if you brought it back in the morning."

I spontaneously reach out and give her a hug. She stands there stiffly before half-heartedly returning the gesture.

"You're very kind," I say.

For the first time since she opened the door, she smiles. "Off you go."

I carry my bags over to the car, wondering if this is a sign that my visit won't be as difficult as I thought.

I sure hope so.

I DRIVE over to the address in Notting Hill, using my phone's GPS to guide me. It turns out Rachel lives in a terrace house, all traditional brick and white rendering. The street is clean, and her place has a blue door, just like in the movie with Hugh Grant and Julia Roberts. Rachel often used to make me watch rom-coms with her, and I'll bet she picked this place specifically because of its location and appearance. I wouldn't have thought it was a cheap area to reside though, so I don't know how she can afford it.

I knock. It takes a moment for Rachel to come to the door, but when she does, the girls are right behind her, squealing in excitement. I instinctively bend down to greet them, ignoring Rachel for the moment. The girls are my priority.

"Daddy! We missed you so much!"

Oh God. I can't handle this, and I feel my eyes welling up. Being able to hug them and give them piggyback rides is something I've missed more than anything.

I wrap an arm around each girl and squeeze them tight. "I missed you two munchkins as well."

Rachel clearly knew I was coming because she doesn't act remotely surprised by my presence.

"Mum told me you were in London," she says, as if reading my mind.

"Thank you for not going out."

She shrugs. "If we'd had plans, we would have."

I force myself not to show how frustrated I am with her. "Would it be okay if I came in for a bit?"

She stands aside and lets me through. I walk down a narrow hall and come out in a chaotic living room. Rachel was never big on cleaning so I used to do most of it. If my time here wasn't so limited, I'd ask to do a quick tidy-up.

"Are you well?" I ask politely as I sit down on the couch, clearing a pile of dolls in the process. The girls immediately jump on top of me and cling tightly.

"I'm all right," she says equally neutrally.

"How are you finding settling in? Are you working?"

She looks down her nose at me. "How am I supposed to work, huh? I have two three-year-olds to look after."

"I wasn't trying to imply anything. I was just wondering how you were getting by. And you mentioned on the phone that the girls were going to pre-school."

"If you must know, Henry owns this place and is letting me and the girls live here."

"Is Henry the girls' biological father?"

She nods.

"Does he live here too?"

"God, no." She wrinkles her nose. "The guy's let himself go completely in the last few years. But he has no choice. He has to provide for the girls."

I simultaneously feel sorry for Henry and intense dislike for the woman in front of me. I wonder if Henry even knew I existed when he slept with Rachel back then.

I know I'm not going to get anywhere by saying what I really think, so I take a moment to formulate my next words.

"My lawyer said your lawyer is taking a bit longer than usual to process our settlement. I was hoping that by coming here and seeing you in person, we could find a resolution that works for everyone."

"I've already explained what I want."

"But please, Rachel, you know I can't accept one weekend a year. It's not fair to the girls or me."

"Why do you want to see them? I thought you'd be glad to be rid of them."

My eyes widen, and I look down at the beautiful creatures snuggled into each of my arms. "Hey, munchkins, would it be okay if your mummy and I had a quick chat alone? And then I promise I'll spend the rest of the day with you."

They reluctantly pull away. "Promise?" Isabella asks.

"Promise," I say.

They wander off, and I frown at Rachel. "I hope you haven't been telling them I don't want to see them."

"I haven't told them anything."

"Have they asked where I am?"

"I just told them you're busy with work."

"Why would you think I'd be glad to be rid of them?"

"Because they're not yours. They're not your responsibility anymore."

"But they are. You made them my responsibility by lying to me for four years! And regardless of the circumstances, I still love them. They're still mine. Please, Rachel, it would kill me to never spend time with them again."

I can't help myself and start crying. Rachel looks uncomfortable but I don't care. She's the one who broke me. She can deal with the fallout.

After a moment, she holds her hands up in surrender. "Fine. We'll figure something out."

"Thank you. I'm willing to be flexible, but I need you to be as well."

She rolls her eyes. "Whatever."

"I'm going to go and see what the girls are doing."

She nods.

I stand and go in search of the twins. I've used up all my self-restraint trying not to yell at Rachel, and now I need to have her out of my sight.

The rest of this trip is about my daughters.

CHAPTER 28

TASH

A week goes by and I don't hear from Lincoln. It feels all too familiar, both from when Brad deserted me, and also like after Lincoln disappeared following our night together. I know he had a lot to process then with his legal stuff, and he supposedly wrote me that text that never arrived, but this time the situation involves me. I know I asked him for space, but I still wish he'd give me a tiny clue as to what he's thinking.

Everything feels so up in the air. One minute I'm convinced he'll choose to give everything up just for the chance to see Isabella and Madison again, and the next I'm hoping he'll realise that I'm carrying his biological child and he has a duty to talk it through. But he has competing priorities: the twins, the possibility of expanding his music career...

Another week begins and my hopes fall further and further. I start considering how I can possibly care for a newborn, a six-year-old, and still keep my business afloat. I need to figure out if I can afford to hire someone to oversee everything, at least part-time.

It's a rainy Monday morning when I arrive home from

dropping Daisy at school and find Lincoln sitting on my doorstep, dripping wet.

I'm annoyed at myself because the first thing I think is how hot he looks, with droplets of water trickling off his curls and his black T-shirt clinging to his chest.

My pulse quickens as I approach. He stands, looking as nervous as I feel.

"Hey," he says softly.

"Hey." I'm not going to give him anything until he makes the first move.

"You look great," he says.

I self-consciously smooth down my hair, which is starting to fade. I've decided to lay off the fluorescent hair colour for the rest of my pregnancy. I know the science isn't conclusive regarding any possible effects it may have on the baby but I figure my head can use a break anyway.

"Thanks," I say neutrally.

He briefly looks at my belly, which is still flat. I know with Daisy, I didn't really start to show until around four or five months, and then I suddenly looked like I had a basketball under my clothes.

"How are you feeling?" he asks. He makes no attempt to come inside, and I can't tell if that's a good or bad thing.

"I'm okay. Feeling a little nauseated, but mostly fine." I point to the front door. "Do you want to come in?"

"Only if that's all right with you?"

"Sure."

I head inside, letting him follow. I don't offer any information from my end. He needs to do some talking first.

I retrieve a towel from the linen cupboard so he can dry off, and then I head to the kitchen to heat up some water. "Do you want anything?" I ask.

"No, thanks."

He doesn't look like he knows whether to sit down or hover,

so he leans against the kitchen counter while I prepare a teabag in a cup.

We briefly make eye contact, and he smiles weakly. "I don't even know where to start."

"At the beginning?"

"You're right. Okay, so I wanted to give you that space you asked for, but it was just so damn hard. I picked up my phone a dozen times a day to call you, but I thought if you asked me to leave you alone, it was for a reason. And I appreciate why you did. It gave me some time to sort out stuff too."

"You mean mentally?"

"Well, yeah, but also in a practical sense. I flew to the UK after you told me the news."

My stomach drops. I gave him too much space, and now he's worked things out with Rachel, and he's here to tell me he's not interested in seeing our child.

He sees my expression and looks appalled. "Wait, no. This is all good. Please let me explain."

My breathing slows a little.

"I went over there because I needed to see the girls and make sure they were okay. I wasn't able to do that before because I was under contract for the tour. But oh God, Tash, it was next to impossible to see them again and then leave."

"How was Rachel?" I ask casually.

"Not easy to deal with, I have to say. But she did seem happier than when we were together. I don't think I ever realised how much she missed her family. Over the years, she mentioned wanting to visit them more often, but we never really had the money. I was hoping that if I won *Sing to Me*, I could pay for a big extended trip for us all to go. As it was, she'd secretly been hiding money away without telling me, which is how she was able to afford it when she took the girls. But after seeing her again, I realised *I* was never really happy. I loved the idea of us, but the reality was hard. We had nothing in common

– at least not in recent years – and she was too good at keeping secrets."

I finish making my tea and take a sip. I stay quiet, letting him finish what he needs to say.

"But you know, whenever I think of you, I feel calm and happy. And I've never once doubted your sincerity. I know the day you told me about the pregnancy, I asked you to confirm whether the baby was mine, but I wasn't really asking because I was worried you were lying. I just needed to hear it a few times to let it sink in."

My heart softens a little. "I know this must be really difficult for you, but I want you to know, I don't expect anything. I'll cope if you decide this isn't something you want to be part of."

He comes over to my side of the counter and grabs my hands. "I *do* want to be part of this. I know it's insanely soon, but I want us to make this work. I really want to be around for this baby. And for you."

My stomach fills with butterflies. "You do?"

"Yes! I'm not a casual hookup kind of guy. When I invited you to Sydney, it was because I wanted to get to know you better. And while I was only starting to get over Rachel, it never once impacted how I felt about you."

"But bringing a baby into this…"

"I know. It's going to be hard. We won't have that long to get to know each other properly before he or she arrives, but we'll deal with the situation we have."

"Are you sure?"

"Yes! Oh, but first, I need to tell you something that happened in London."

The butterflies scatter. I'm getting emotional whiplash the way my mood is flying back and forth. My first instinct is to think that even though he said he's not a casual hookup kind of guy, he's about to admit he got drunk one night and slept with some random woman while he was away.

"What happened in London?"

"I convinced Rachel to let me bring the girls back to Australia for a few weeks several times a year. And once they start school, it'll be most holidays."

He looks at me guardedly, waiting for my reaction.

"Oh! Wow! That's amazing news!"

He smiles the first genuinely happy smile I've seen from him in ages. "You're okay with that?"

"Why wouldn't I be?"

"I don't know. Because it makes things even crazier?"

"Lincoln. These are your girls, whether biologically or not. For you to be able to see them again in a meaningful way is fantastic."

He pulls me in and wraps his arms tightly around me. "Damn, Tash. I think you are quite possibly the perfect woman."

"I wouldn't go that far." I laugh. "But if you insist, I'll take it."

He cups my chin with his hands and gently kisses me. "I can't wait to see what the future holds for us. It's going to be a wild ride. But I'm ready."

"I feel exactly the same way."

CHAPTER 29

LINCOLN

To say I'm overwhelmed is an understatement.

In the space of a few months, I've lost the woman I thought I would spend my life with, discovered my twin daughters aren't biologically mine, met an incredible woman who made me realise the true meaning of a decent human being, and almost lost *her* because I was too wrapped up in my own crap to properly consider what she was going through.

But now we're expecting a child together, and I've gone from being on my own to suddenly having the twins back in my life, as well as Tash and Daisy.

Not to mention Tash's friend Millicent and her son Ryder, who I didn't quite appreciate how deeply embedded in Tash's life they were until now.

But I'm starting to adjust.

I think the twins must have worn Rachel down because she's agreed to let me chat with them via Zoom a few times a week. I'm not sure she would have voluntarily made that decision but she's finally allowed it. And she seemed to feel sorry for me and went back to only wanting half the proceeds from the sale of our house. I think she realised that when I found out she was taking advantage of another man's finances, I could possibly use that against her if we were to go to court.

Still, there's a long way to go on this journey. It's going to be a few more days before Tash can get the paternity test done, and I'd be lying if I said I wasn't freaking out about it. I do trust Tash, but I trusted Rachel too, and I hate myself for not being able to shut off the tiny part of my brain that's questioning the outcome.

Not that Tash has any idea about that. I know expressing my doubts aloud would only make things more complicated. I'm just going to have to suck it up for a bit longer.

And today, I'm proving my commitment by going with Tash to visit her parents. She wants to break the pregnancy news in person, so I offered to accompany her. And while Daisy already knows what's going on, we're leaving her with Millicent for the day. Tash is worried her parents might not react favourably to the news, especially since I haven't met them yet.

I pull up at her place, where she's already waiting out the front. She climbs into the passenger seat, and I kiss her on the cheek. "You look beautiful."

She smiles shyly. "I feel like a whale already."

"I don't know how you can say that. You look the same as always to me. Which is absolutely perfect."

We drive in the direction of Eight Mile Plains, where Tash's parents live. Apparently they've been in the same house since before Tash was born.

"How are you feeling otherwise? You mentioned you had a little nausea a while back."

"Thankfully that's subsided. I remember with Daisy, I only had it right at the beginning, so fingers crossed it stays away."

"I remember with Rachel, she had it really bad…" I trail off, wondering if it's appropriate to mention my ex's pregnancy.

Tash notices my hesitation. "Hey, it's okay. Please feel free to talk about Rachel whenever you need to. I'm actually glad you have experience with kids. You know what you're letting yourself in for."

I laugh. "I love kids. To me, any of the craziness is offset by all the fun you can have. And just so you know, I did my fair share of getting up during the night, so I'm not completely delusional."

She raises an eyebrow. "We'll have to wait and see if you feel the same way once this one comes along."

We hit a bit of traffic, but the time goes quickly. Despite the seriousness of what we're facing, I'm happy to just be hanging out with this gorgeous woman. Before I knew she was pregnant, I was excited at the opportunity to have a proper relationship with her. That hasn't changed. Obviously there's a little more pressure to make it work, but I've never shied away from a challenge.

We arrive in a suburban street, and Tash directs me to a single-storey red-brick house.

I get out of the car and go over to Tash's side to open her door and help her out. She giggles. "Such a gentleman."

She squeezes my arm, and I can see a trace of apprehension in her eyes. "Are you ready for this?"

"Yep. Are you?"

She lets out a puff of air. "I think so."

We walk hand in hand from the driveway to the door. Tash knocks before trying the handle and finding it unlocked. I follow her inside.

"Hello?" she calls out.

"In here," a woman's voice responds from somewhere out the back.

We head down the hall and come out in a bright kitchen overlooking the yard. A woman who looks a lot like Tash – minus the colourful hair – is pouring water into a jug, and an older man, presumably Tash's dad, is retrieving glasses from a cupboard.

Tash's mum places the jug on the counter and comes over to

give her a hug. "Darling! It's good to see you."

"You too, Mum."

Her mum steps away and appraises me. "You look familiar. Where do I know you from?"

Tash laughs. "Don't tell me you watch *Sing to Me* as well."

Her eyes widen. "Lincoln Page?"

"The one and only," I say, grinning.

"What are you doing here?"

"We're dating, Mum," Tash says awkwardly.

"Oh. Wow." She looks around. "And where's Daisy?"

"She's having a playdate with Ryder. You know what those two are like. I couldn't drag her away," Tash fibs.

"Well, then." Her mum comes over and also gives me a hug. "It's lovely to meet you, Lincoln. I'm Keiko. And this is Tash's father, Dennis."

"It's great to meet you both too," I say, suddenly aware that this is probably the politest they'll be today. I can't imagine many parents responding with delight at the news their daughter is pregnant to a guy they just met.

Dennis shakes my hand and ushers us outside to a covered patio area.

Keiko pours us water and focuses on me. "I really enjoyed your performances on TV."

"Thank you."

"If memory serves me correctly, didn't you have a wife and two daughters?"

"Uh, we weren't married, but yes, I did have a partner." I still struggle to say all this out loud, but I know I have to. "She moved to England with the girls, who, it turns out, weren't mine."

Keiko and Dennis exchange a look I can't read.

"Lincoln is still present in their lives," Tash adds. "They'll be coming back during school holidays, and he'll visit them over there occasionally."

"I'm very sorry to hear you've experienced such a difficult

situation," Keiko says. "This all couldn't have happened very long ago. *Sing to Me* only finished in April."

"That's right. It was just after I left the show."

"And you feel ready to enter into another relationship?"

I glance at Tash. She looks as if she'd hoped there'd be more time before breaking the news, but I can see the resignation on her face.

"Yes, I believe so. I care very deeply about your daughter."

Tash wrings her hands together. "Mum, Dad, I was going to wait for a bit to tell you, but since we're already sort of talking about it, I have some news."

"Don't tell me you're pregnant," Keiko jokes.

Tash looks at her unwaveringly. "I am."

Keiko's eyes widen. "No! Really?"

I sneak a peek at Dennis. He's looking at me with narrowed eyes.

"It was unplanned but I'm taking full responsibility," I say.

Keiko shakes her head. "I can't believe you're pregnant."

"I know it's a lot to take in, Mum, but I wanted you and Dad to know as soon as possible. Lincoln and I are going to make this work."

"Do you plan on marrying my daughter?" Keiko demands.

"Mum! We've only just started dating," Tash answers for me. "We're not going to rush into marriage."

"But what's going to stop him from skipping out like that other waste of space you were involved with?"

"I'm not going to skip out," I assure Keiko.

Dennis hadn't talked until now but suddenly pipes up. "Lincoln, why don't you and I go get lunch started while the girls talk?"

"Sure."

I follow Dennis inside and watch as he gets out a breadboard and a knife. I almost make a joke about not having sharp objects nearby but decide I don't know him well enough yet.

He hands me a baguette, which I start cutting up while he gets some cheese, tomatoes and cucumbers from the fridge.

"I assume you know the full story of what happened with Daisy's father?" he says.

"Actually, Tash hasn't told me the details. Just that he left before she was born."

"Yeah, well, there was a bit more to it than that."

I put the knife down. "What happened?"

"Brad was the kind of guy who only looked out for himself. He treated my daughter like a trophy and wore her down until she lost all her spark. To be honest, I was glad when he left, because it was the first time I got to see some of Tash's fire again."

"I'm so sorry." It makes me sad to think about Tash suffering in any way.

"He had an oversized ego and was always bragging to me about how he was on the verge of some large payday. The problem was, nothing ever eventuated, and in the meantime, he was sponging off my daughter. She supported him financially throughout their entire relationship."

"And you think I'm going to be the same."

"The music business isn't exactly known for its reliable pay."

"Actually, I just came off a national tour, which gave me a fairly decent salary. I also play regular gigs, and when things are slow, I work as a barista. I do whatever I have to do. I'm not fussy."

Dennis nods thoughtfully. "That's good to hear. What about your parents? What do they think of your career choice?"

"They're not fans," I say flatly.

"You're not close?"

"You could say that." The last thing I thought I'd be doing is confiding in my girlfriend's father about my parents' total absence in my life.

"You want to talk about it?"

"Let's just say they like their alcohol."

"It sounds like you've had to deal with a lot in your life too."

Tell me about it. And if your daughter's child doesn't turn out to be mine, I may not recover.

"What can you do?" I say, shrugging.

Dennis finishes compiling the sandwiches and hands me the tray.

"Just keep on doing what you're doing."

I half smile. I'll take that to mean I'm on my way to getting the guy's tick of approval.

§✿

LATER IN THE CAR, thoughts are swirling around in my brain. While the rest of the afternoon went smoothly, the fact that Keiko asked if I was prepared to marry Tash freaked me out a little. I haven't even told her I love her yet. It's so early, and there's so much up in the air, I can't make sense of my feelings.

I definitely didn't lie when I said I cared deeply about her, but love is such a strong word, and the last person I loved completely crushed me.

"How are you feeling?" Tash asks.

"It's a lot," I say honestly.

"I know. But we knew that going in. You were amazing today. Thank you for coming."

"No problem."

"Is there anything you want to talk about?" she asks.

"I don't think so. I just need to work through a few things in my head."

"Well, if you change your mind, I'm here."

"Thank you." And then I feel terrible. Tash is likely going through the same thing as me. Maybe worse.

When we get back to her place, she turns to me hopefully. "You want to come in for a bit?"

"Actually, I might go home. The girls will be on Zoom soon,

and I don't want to miss them."

She nods, but I can tell she's a little disappointed. I just can't summon the energy right now to be the guy she needs.

"I'll call you tomorrow," I say.

She strokes my face before she leaves. "Take care."

I watch her go inside before I drive away.

But I feel like everything is wrong.

On returning to my place, I head straight for the living room and throw myself on the couch.

I shouldn't be here alone. I should be there with Tash and Daisy. Being invited to go and hang out temporarily at their house has made me realise how separate we still are. How are we supposed to have a child and a normal relationship?

I don't like how we left things. And I have higher standards for myself than to run away when things get tough.

I jump in the car and drive all the way back over to Highgate Hill. I stride up the front path and knock firmly on the door.

She answers, surprised. "What are you–"

I cut her off by pulling her in close and kissing her firmly. It takes a moment, but I feel her body soften as she kisses me back. I run my fingers through her hair and inhale her beautiful strawberry-scented perfume.

I gently pull away and look at her intently. "I just needed to see you one more time today."

She smiles. "I'm glad you did."

"If that invitation still stands, I'd like to come in."

"Of course. We're just going to get take-out tonight and watch some more Disney. How do you feel about Hawaiian pizza and *Moana?*"

"Sounds like heaven. The twins haven't called yet, but when they do, I might have to briefly sneak away to talk to them. Is that okay?"

Tash kisses me on the neck and yanks me inside.

"Of course, you gorgeous man."

CHAPTER 30

TASH

$\mathcal{T}$he next few days are crazy. I'm busy working, and Lincoln has a bunch of stuff to go through with his band. It's looking more and more like a formal deal with Max is imminent, and I'm so excited for him. I don't want to jinx myself, but I feel like everything is finally coming together.

I know Lincoln is still secretly worried about the results of the paternity test, but I have a surprise for him.

It's 6pm on a Wednesday when I go to his place. I told him I had a meeting, which is technically true, but not for what he thinks.

As soon as I get inside, he comes to greet me, picking me up and swinging me around.

I laugh. "You won't be able to do that for much longer."

He places me gently on the floor in the hall. "Nonsense. How did your meeting go?"

"Good." I can barely contain my excitement.

"Is everything okay?"

"Yes! Kind of. Damn. I was going to try to be all cool about it, but I can't."

He stares at me. "What's going on?"

I hold up an envelope. "The doctor had a cancellation a few days ago, and I managed to get the paternity test done early. The results are in here."

Lincoln's eyes widen. "What? Why didn't you tell me? I was going to go with you to the appointment."

"I know, I know. But you were freaking out about it so much, I thought I'd go and get it over with, and we could do this bit together."

He looks at the envelope as if it's about to bite him. He ushers me through to the living room, and we sit down. "So how do you want to do this?"

I hold out the envelope. "I want you to open it. I already know what it's going to say, so you should do the honours."

"Are you sure?"

"Yes. I've said from the beginning, I want us to be upfront with each other. We've both gone through crappy relationships, so we have to make sure we're being as open and respectful of each other as possible."

He reaches out and holds my hand. "Have I told you lately how amazing you are?"

"Probably. But I never get tired of hearing it," I say, smiling.

He gently takes the envelope from me and holds it for a moment.

"It's going to be okay," I whisper.

He kisses me on the mouth. "I know."

He slowly runs his finger along the side of the envelope to reveal its contents. And even though I know the outcome, it feels like everything's happening in slow motion.

This is it.

He unfolds the report, and I see his eyes skim for the relevant information. I peer over his shoulder and see a table with a bunch of codes down the left, and two columns to its right – one with the baby's information and one with Lincoln's. None of it makes much sense except for the line at the bottom: Probability of Paternity.

99.9998%.

Lincoln stands, whooping with delight and grabbing my hands. He pulls me to my feet and hugs me tightly. "It's ours!"

"Ha-ha, easy, buddy. Our child is getting squished."

He quickly loosens his grip and then kneels in front of me. I'm wearing a skirt with a black tank top, and he slowly lifts the top to expose my belly. He looks at it for a moment and then leans forward to cover my skin in little feathery kisses.

I giggle and ruffle his hair. "That tickles."

He looks up at me, smiling.

"There's something else," I say.

He looks stricken. "Oh God. It's twins, isn't it?"

I cackle with laughter. "No! Jeez. Could you imagine having two sets of twins in your life? I was going to say you may have missed a small detail on the report."

He looks at me, confused. "What?"

"Turn it over."

He obliges and makes a choking sound. "The report tells us the baby's gender?"

"And that might be...?" I gesture my hand in a hurry-up motion.

"Wait, you don't know yet?"

"No. I told you, I wanted us to do this together. Come on. Don't keep me in suspense!"

"It's a boy!"

I tear up. "A boy!" I lean down and place my hands on either side of Lincoln's face. "One more thing."

"I don't think I can take much more."

"This is important. Once the baby's born, I'd like you to register the birth certificate for us."

He looks me in the eye. "Thank you for being the kindest, most patient, and overall awesome human being I know."

Tears are rolling freely down my face. "The same goes for you."

He holds me again, this time more softly, and we stay there for a long time, lost in the moment.

But then I pull away and give him a cheeky smile. "You know, I don't have to pick up Daisy for at least an hour."

He chuckles. "And you're telling me this, because?"

I grab his hand and pull him towards the bedroom.

"What do you think?"

He lets me lead the way.

Today is a great day.

CHAPTER 31

LINCOLN

*L*ife is wonderful. Not only am I soon to become a father to a little boy, but I've also been able to reconnect with my daughters and establish the start of an amazing relationship with Tash and *her* daughter. And the icing on the cake? Today, the guys and I have a meeting with Max. He's flown up from Sydney, apparently to see JC, but he wanted to check in with us too.

He's asked to meet us at Brew in the Queen Street Mall, so we order beers while we wait for him to show up.

I love my guys. What I thought was something that would never progress beyond a pub band is now doing better than anything I could have ever imagined. Our recent national tour has been the highlight of our professional career so far.

And the fact that we've been able to transition into doing our own music so smoothly is something I could never have dreamed of.

Max arrives, and he waves to us while he orders a beer before coming over to join us in the corner.

"How's it going, lads?" he asks, sitting down and taking a sip of his drink.

"Good, thanks," I say. The other guys nod in agreement.

"Well, that was all very limp and uninspired. I'm hoping what I'm about to say will change that tune."

I look at him, confused. I'd thought this was just an obligatory visit on the way to see JC.

"I've been talking to the team at Intergalactic and negotiated a deal for you. Three albums, plus a world tour."

He leans back and puts his hands behind his head, a huge grin on his face.

It takes a moment for it to sink in. My brain short-circuits as I process the full meaning of those words.

And then suddenly it's like a dam has burst, and all four of us stand to hug each other. I slap the guys on the back and shake each of their hands.

"Holy shit," Beau says. "Is this for real?"

"Yep." Max also stands so he's eye-level with us. "We're already looking at the itinerary. You're going to be on the festival circuit as well as headlining your own shows in over twenty countries. In the US alone, we're looking at more than fifty gigs."

I can't comprehend this. This is the ultimate. We've made it. We've really made it.

And then something occurs to me.

"Do you know the timing yet?"

"It's all still in flux but we're getting you into the studio in Sydney in a couple of weeks to start laying down some tunes. The label has some ideas for the track list..."

"Will we have any input into what goes on the album?" I check.

"Yes, yes, of course. But don't worry about that now. This is the good part! Enjoy it!"

"When would the tour start?"

"Again, that's still all up in the air, but we're developing an entire strategy involving singles, marketing, and then getting you on the road ASAP. I'd say probably in about three or four months?"

I frown. That'll be near the end of Tash's pregnancy.

"You know Tash and I are having a baby soon…"

He waves a hand dismissively. "And? Musicians have kids all the time. Bring 'em along. Or leave 'em at home. Either way, it's not a big deal."

I beg to differ. This child is a huge deal. And Tash is a huge deal. This needs to work for her too.

The other guys are still all toasting each other and ordering stronger drinks, even though it's only two in the afternoon. I know none of them have kids, so it's easy for them to get excited.

I need to talk to Tash.

"Do you mind if I head out for a bit?" I say. "I can meet you back here in an hour, or wherever you're going to be. I just want to tell Tash the news in person."

"It's your call, man," Max says. "But usually, my newly signed clients want to hang around and celebrate for a while."

"I do want to celebrate. But…"

"It's okay. I get it. Go to your woman. Call us when you're done."

"Thanks," I say gratefully. I quickly tell the other guys what I'm doing and take off.

Tash should be at home. Although by the time I get there she might have had to leave for the afternoon school pickup.

I'm right, and when I arrive at Highgate Hill, there's no answer at the door. It's only then I realise Tash has never given me a spare key to her house.

And she doesn't have one for mine either.

While I wait for them to return, I drive over to the nearest mall and have a key cut for my place, also buying a little key cap shaped like a panda as a reminder of the rice balls she made for me the day she rescued me from the paparazzi. That seems like a lifetime ago now.

It gets me thinking about the other encounters we had. It's quite strange thinking back on when we hung out in Sydney before Rachel and I split up. I could appreciate Tash was a special person even then, but obviously I didn't see her in a romantic way until later.

Still, a tiny part of me feels guilty that I did know Tash before my relationship with Rachel was over. But I would *never* have acted on any attraction if Rachel hadn't left.

I head back to Tash's and pull up just as she's arriving with Daisy. I jump out of the car and give them both a hug.

"Hey, my gorgeous girls."

Daisy blushes. I think she's still getting used to having me in her life. She wouldn't have had many older male influences apart from Tash's dad, so I can understand it would be an adjustment.

She runs ahead, grabbing the key from Tash and unlocking the front door.

"I have something you might want to add to that keyring," I say before we head inside. I hold out the panda key.

Tash looks down, uncomprehendingly at first. And then the light dawns. "Is this…"

I nod, smiling. "I know the place is on the market, but until it sells, I want you to feel as comfortable at my house as you do here."

She takes the key from my hand and encloses it in her own. "Thank you." She rummages around in her handbag. "I actually had this made up ages ago and was trying to figure out the right time to give it to you." She hands me a key too.

I laugh. "Really?"

"Yes! I mean, I was initially thinking we'd keep our separate places so Daisy could get used to everything, but I don't want you to ever feel unwelcome."

I pull her close. "I love you, Natasha Northwood."

She runs her fingers through my hair and sighs. "I love you too, Lincoln Page."

She presses her lips to mine, and if it weren't for her daughter's presence inside, I would be dragging Tash to the bedroom.

I beam. "And I haven't even told you the craziest part of today."

She points inside. "Why don't we continue this in the living room?"

I nod and head in. Daisy has disappeared off somewhere. I sit Tash down on the couch and take her hands. "I just came from a meeting with Max. We've been offered a three-album deal and a world tour."

"Oh my God!" She squeezes my fingers so tightly the circulation is almost cut off. "This is it!"

"I know!" And then I turn serious. "But you know what it means..."

She thinks for a second. "Oh, right. Lots of you being away. Do you know the timing yet?"

"Not exactly. But I have to go to Sydney in two weeks for a month, and that's just the start." I look at her earnestly. "I'll do everything I can to make this work for us. I'll still come to as many doctor appointments as possible, and I'll force my lawyer to put in a clause so I'm back here for the birth."

Her eyes sparkle. "You're the sweetest person I have ever known, Lincoln Page."

"So you're okay with this?"

"Of course I am! This is your dream! We both get to have our dreams!"

I finally let myself relax a little. I should have known Tash would react like this. She's one of my biggest fans.

"I'm so lucky."

"No, *I'm* lucky. And to think, if I hadn't gone to Nicky's Bar that night, I wouldn't have made friends with Felix, and none of this would have happened."

"I know. I guess it was meant to be."

She blushes.

"What?"

"I… probably shouldn't tell you this, but I saw Felix invite you to Nicky's on Instagram, and that's why I was there."

I gently poke her in the ribs. "Were you stalking me?"

"No! All right, maybe. I realised as soon as I arrived that I wasn't actually going to approach you if I saw you, but then you found me. Still, I did watch you every week on *Sing to Me*, so yeah, I probably verged on being a stalker."

I pull her against me again and rest my chin on her head. "I guess it just took a while for the timing to work out. I don't want to take away from anything I had with Rachel, but in hindsight, my relationship with her was nothing compared to what I have with you."

Tash kisses my chest. "That means more to me than you can possibly imagine."

I smile and lean back on the couch, my arms still wrapped around her.

I don't think things could possibly get any better.

CHAPTER 32

TASH

*L*ater that evening, I'm making some dinner, and Lincoln is helping me. I've decided to teach him how to make proper ramen. Traditional Japanese ramen is made with animal stock but I did a little research and found a broth I could make with soy sauce, miso paste and dried shitake mushrooms.

Lincoln is already a pretty good cook but he never seemed to experiment with anything fancy.

He'd gone back to see the guys for a couple of hours this afternoon but said he couldn't bear to be away from me, Daisy and the baby.

"I told Max we can't do any shows two weeks before the birth or four weeks after," he tells me.

"And he was okay with that?"

"Not particularly. But he said he'd do whatever he could to make it happen."

"If you can get *any* time off around the birth, I'd appreciate it."

He kisses me on the forehead. "You're the cutest." And then he seems to remember something. He excitedly gets out his phone and shows me the screen. "We got our final pay from the last tour today."

I look at the number, squinting for a moment, and then I stare at him, shocked. "Are you serious?"

"And there's going to be so much more where that came from. We'll be able to buy a mansion anywhere we want after this next tour is over."

My heart almost bursts with happiness. And not because of the money. It's because Lincoln is finally seeing the benefits of following his dreams. "I'm so proud of you."

"You know what this means?"

"What?"

"That you can wind back your business. Take the pressure off."

My face hardens. "Sorry, what?"

"I mean, you don't have to kill yourself running this huge business while looking after a newborn."

I bite my bottom lip. "I'm not *killing* myself running the business. And I have no intention of winding it back."

He looks at me, confused. "I didn't mean anything by it. I just thought–"

"Nope, you didn't think. I've worked really hard to get where I am, and I want to succeed in my own career. I don't need you to look after me or make me feel like all I'm good for is being a trophy wife... staying home with the baby and doing all the housework."

His eyes widen. "That's not what I was implying at all. You know I'm not like that..."

"You're sure sounding like it. The world doesn't revolve around you, you know."

"I never said it did!"

"If we're going to make this work, we have to operate as a team. And especially once your tour is over, you're going to have to be the one to suck it up and do more of the house stuff."

"Of course. That was never in question. Please, Tash, you're making me feel like the bad guy here."

"How do you think *I* feel? Keeping you away from your precious tour for six weeks because of the baby? Making you sacrifice all these things for me?"

"It's not a sacrifice! I want to be with you and the kids. Touring is a means to an end. And yes, I enjoy it, but I won't if I know you're not happy. The four of us are what is most important right now."

"What about Isabella and Madison?"

"What about them?"

"How are they supposed to fit into your tour schedule? Is it going to be left up to me to babysit them if it's school holidays and you're still on tour?"

"No! Jesus! Tash! This is getting way out of control. I'll organise the girls separately. Please don't worry about that."

I suddenly feel deflated. "I'm sorry. I just feel like there's too much going on, and I'm going to be the one to suffer."

He quickly steps forward, wrapping me in a hug. "You will *not* suffer. I will make sure that doesn't happen."

"I hope so."

Lincoln

I LEAVE SOON AFTER DINNER. The ramen was delicious, but the vibe was weird. Tash was quiet, and every time I tried to bring up the topic of her work again, she shut me down.

I really didn't mean any harm by what I said, and if I'm being honest, I feel like she overreacted a little.

When I get home, I call Felix. It's times like these when I wish he lived nearby. Talking on the phone isn't quite the same.

"Hey, buddy," he says. "How's world domination coming along?"

"Really good, actually. Although there was a slight hiccup today."

"Do you want to tell me about the good stuff or the hiccup first?"

"Uh, I guess they're part of the same issue, so both?"

"Go ahead."

"Okay, so Max confirmed today he's signing the band permanently, and we've got a deal with Intergalactic Records."

"Link! That's fantastic!"

"I know. It means a three-album contract and a world tour."

"I knew you'd get there. Well done! But what's the hiccup?"

"I suggested to Tash that she could wind back her business a little now that I'm earning more, and she has the baby coming."

Felix is quiet for a second.

"What?" I ask self-consciously.

"You told an artist to stop doing what she loves?"

"It wasn't like that! I was trying to help! If *I* was given the opportunity to take things easy, I would."

"But would you, really? If you didn't have the impending birth of your child to consider, you can't tell me you wouldn't be itching to get into the studio immediately and then take off on an international tour."

"I…" Damn it. He's right. All I wanted to do was make sure Tash wasn't overwhelmed, but instead I've made her feel like what she does doesn't matter.

And then I think about how Daisy's dad treated her, and I feel even worse. He was always putting her second too.

Felix astutely understands my silence. "Fortunately for you, Tash is an amazing girl, and she will forgive you as soon as you apologise properly. I'm thinking chocolates, a foot rub and a bath full of rose petals."

I chuckle weakly. "Jeez. Life's crazy."

"But really, shouldn't you be enjoying the ride? Your career is about to go into the stratosphere, you have a hot awesome woman who is pregnant with your child..."

"...and I'll get to see Isabella and Madison again soon. Rachel finally agreed to let me see them properly."

"See? This is the dream, buddy! Make the most of it."

I mentally shake myself. "Hey, enough about me. What's new with you?"

"Oh, the usual. But I *am* a finalist for a prestigious art award down here. I find out next week if my work will be displayed alongside some of my idols. Plus there's a not-so-small sum of money involved."

"That's amazing, Felix! You deserve to win. Your art is so, so good. And what about everything else? How's the love life?"

Felix laughs. "You never ask me about my love life."

"You normally tell me if you're seeing anyone but I haven't heard you mention a soul for months."

"I've sort of just started seeing this guy called Ames. He works as a tour guide at the Museum of Contemporary Art. It's early days, which is why I hadn't told you about him yet."

"Oh, I'm really happy for you. Have you showed him your stuff?"

"We actually met when I was talking to the director there. Ames was just coming off a tour and asked if he could have a look at my work. And the rest is history."

"Sounds like your life is pretty well sorted for now. I just have to get mine back on track too."

"You will. Tash is nothing like Rachel. She's worth fighting for."

"I know. It feels different this time, Felix. Deeper. More meaningful."

"Now aren't you glad I befriended her at Nicky's that night?"

"Actually, she told me that she saw your message on Instagram earlier that day, and that's why she was there."

Felix roars with laughter. "Is that so? Well, I still get to take credit."

"You can do that. Thanks for being such a great friend. I hope we can see more of each other in the future."

"We will. I was thinking of coming up for a few months next year. Maybe rent out my house temporarily or something."

"That would be awesome."

"Anyway, I have to go. I'm meeting Ames for dinner."

"Have fun!"

I hang up, feeling better already. I was such an idiot. And while my heart was in the right place, I still need to use my brain before opening my mouth.

I'm going to make this right.

I check the time. It's pretty late and I'm not sure Tash would appreciate me rocking up on her doorstep at 10pm on a weeknight, even if it was to apologise.

I'll make sure I go there first thing.

I love that woman and I want her to be glad that we're starting a family together. Because, despite how insane everything is, I wouldn't want it any other way.

CHAPTER 33

TASH

I am so disappointed. How could Lincoln think my career doesn't matter? Does he just imagine I'm playing around and biding my time until I find a rich husband who can do everything for me?

I'm reminded of when I dated Brad and how he used to always act like I was a second-class citizen. And even though I was the one earning the money, his interests always took priority.

I refuse to put myself in a situation like that ever again. But I worry that with Lincoln signing a recording deal and going on an international tour, I'll have to fit around him.

I text Millicent.

> I'm feeling sad. Can you come over?

> On my way. Bringing ice cream.

I smile. Millicent is by far the best friend anyone could ever have. Maybe I *should* buy her an Audi after all.

It's getting late, and I wonder if she's going to bring Ryder with her. I feel bad that I just expect her to drop everything at a moment's notice.

But when she arrives, she's alone. And thankfully holding a cooler bag that I assume contains ice cream.

"Thanks so much for coming. Where's the boy?"

"Still with his dad. They're coming back from a fishing trip up north and won't be back until tomorrow. Never mind that Ryder's supposed to be at school by 8.45am."

"It must be hard dealing with a difficult ex."

She pushes her way inside and dumps the bag on the kitchen counter. "Yeah, Nate can be infuriating sometimes, but I have to say, he's a good dad. Ryder adores him. I never know if they're going to come back alive from whatever adventure Nate takes them on but they seem to spend a lot of quality time together."

I open the bag and pull out the ice cream. It's Ben & Jerry's – the same flavour I ate while watching Lincoln on TV the night he was eliminated. A confusing mix of emotions flows through my brain.

"Okay, so what do we need the ice cream therapy for?" Millicent asks.

"Lincoln told me I could wind my business back because he's all fancy and famous now."

She snorts. "I think you're going to have to elaborate slightly."

I get a couple of spoons, handing Millicent one and digging the other straight into the container. I don't have time for bowls tonight.

"He scored a three-album deal and an international world tour."

"How dare he!" she teases.

"Missy! Of course that's amazing, and I'm really excited for him, but what annoyed me was when he showed me the last pay he got, and he was all 'Now you don't have to work anymore, and I can have all the fun while you stay home with the kids'."

Millicent raises an eyebrow. "Did he word it that way exactly?"

"It's what he implied!"

"Okay, hang on. Let's just slow down for a second. Your hot rockstar boyfriend comes home with the most exciting news a person can have. He sees his pregnant girlfriend and wants to make sure she's happy and relaxed... and somehow that's a problem?"

I punch her in the arm. "Don't say it like that. You make me sound like a psycho."

"If Constantinos and I had been together for six months and he came to me saying he'd basically won the lottery and suggested he'd pay for me to work whatever hours I wanted, I'd jump at the chance."

"But that's not the point! I don't want Lincoln's money. I want my own! And I love what I do. If I could, I would do *more* hours."

She nods. "I totally get it. No one's forcing you to give up work or do anything you don't want. But I think you need to cut Lincoln some slack. He was just excited. He probably didn't mean anything by it."

I sigh. "I know. It's just... I want everything to be equal. And I'm worried it won't be in reality."

"I think you need to talk to him about your fears, but also don't get mad at him for wanting to take care of you."

"You're right." I shove a large spoonful of ice cream in my mouth, ignoring the fact it could spill out as I'm talking. "He's kind of the perfect guy, Missy. And he loves me."

"Aw, that's adorable. You make me sick, you're so sweet together."

"I know." Suddenly, I'm a gloopy mess. I really love Lincoln. And not just the guy I idolised on TV. The real him. And I know he's gone through a lot recently but he's still holding it together and trying to make sure I'm happy.

"I should call him."

"He can wait until tomorrow. I'm here now, so we're going to have a girly night. At least, whatever's left of it."

"Yeah, you're right. I think it'll be best if we start afresh tomorrow."

"Let's take this ice cream into the living room, shall we? I feel like watching something violent."

I laugh. "Why violent?"

"I don't know. All this sappiness is making me feel strange. Give me some true crime. Or maybe a creepy serial killer series."

I roll my eyes. "Has anyone ever told you you're a little different?"

"All the time."

"Okay. Excessive violence it is."

We sit down, and I switch on the TV, first making sure Daisy's bedroom door is closed so she won't be disturbed.

My life is pretty damn good.

CHAPTER 34

LINCOLN

I don't sleep that well, but it's not because I'm worried about Tash not forgiving me. I suppose that does play in the back of my mind a little, but it's more because I want to make sure I do and say the right thing when I see her again.

As soon as the shops open, I go and buy everything Felix suggested, including chocolates, roses, and a fancy massage oil, so I can give Tash a foot rub. I'm not sure if she'll opt to leave the petals on the stems or let me put them in the bath for her later, but either way, I'm down with whatever she wants.

I head over to her house afterwards, knowing Daisy should be at school. I have my spare key with me, but I decide it's best to knock.

There's no answer.

Huh. That's not ideal.

I knock again to be on the safe side.

Still no one comes to the door.

I suppose I should try out my new key, just in case they slept in this morning.

I let myself in. "Good morning! Anyone home?"

Silence. A cold feeling settles in my chest. This is all too familiar. The idea of having upset Tash so much that she had to leave her own house to avoid me is devastating.

I check my watch. Almost 10am.

I head into the kitchen and look around. There are breakfast dishes in the sink. That calms me a little. And I shouldn't expect her to be home twenty-four seven. People have errands to run. Like buying groceries. Or visiting the post office.

I get out my phone and dial her number.

It goes to messages.

I have to admit, that doesn't feel good. Adrenaline shoots around my veins, causing my heart rate to spike. I know it seems a little invasive, but I have to know. I run over to Tash's bedroom and yank open the closet door.

Okay. Her clothes are still there. At least most of them. I'd have no idea if she'd removed a handful to tide her over while she stayed elsewhere.

Why don't I have Millicent's number? I don't even know her last name! She's been involved in my life for long enough that I should know these things, but I couldn't even tell you the suburb where she lived.

I go back to the kitchen, scanning for clues like a woefully inadequate private investigator. The counter has three used cups on it. What does that mean? Did the third cup belong to Millicent? Or some guy?

No. That would be crazy. Tash isn't the kind of person to go out and hook up with someone else out of revenge. Is she?

No, she wouldn't. She's pregnant with my child.

Oh God. What if something happened to the baby? But wouldn't Tash let me know? And if she was incapable, the hospital would call, surely?

This is killing me. I think I'm having an anxiety attack. I'm no stranger to those these days.

I call Felix. "Hey, man. Have you heard from Tash this morning?"

"No, why?"

"She's not at home, and she's not answering her phone."

"Maybe she went to have her hair done or something."

"Hey, yeah, that's possible."

"Don't get ahead of yourself. You know this isn't the same as what happened with Rachel."

My throat feels tight. "But what if it is?"

"It isn't. Take a few deep breaths and relax. I'm sure she'll get in touch soon."

"You're right." I do as he says and attempt to regulate my breathing.

"Are you okay?" Felix checks.

"Nope. But hopefully I will be any minute. Can you let me know if she contacts you?"

"Of course. And you let me know once you've spoken to her."

"Will do. Thanks, buddy."

I hang up, still feeling horrible. I have to know what's going on.

My phone rings, and I dive on it.

"Hello? Tash?"

"Yeah, hi. I just thought you should know, I'm at the hospital."

My stomach drops. "What happened?"

"It's Daisy. I think everything'll be okay but I'm still waiting for confirmation."

I hear the panic in her voice. My heart breaks. "I'm coming over. Stay on the line and talk to me."

She starts crying. "There was so much blood."

"Where? How?" I feel sick hearing these details out of context. I look around the house as I head towards the front door, but I don't see any blood.

"She was out playing on the swing set in the yard this morning, and somehow she came off the swing and sliced her arm open on a piece of sheet metal. It had been propped up on the fence since we moved in, and I'd been meaning to get rid of it, and…" She dissolves into more sobs.

"I'm sure it'll be all right. I'll be there soon. Text me exactly where to meet you."

"Okay. Thanks, Lincoln. I'm not sure I'm capable of multi-tasking, so I'll hang up and see you soon."

"I'll be there in a few minutes." I shove my phone in my pocket and hurry out to the car.

I may have sounded confident on the phone but I'm just as terrified for Daisy as Tash.

It's situations like these that really bring your priorities into focus.

Tash, Daisy, and the unborn baby are my family now.

I need to look after them.

CHAPTER 35

TASH

J sit in the waiting room, chewing off what remains of my fingernails. I've always bitten them, but it gets bad when I'm stressed. And this situation is more stressful than nearly any other I've ever faced.

The vision of Daisy holding her arm in the yard as blood dripped onto the grass will be seared into my memory forever. It was like something out of a horror movie.

She didn't even seem to be in that much pain but I knew if we didn't stop the bleeding, things could get dicey.

Millicent had gone home around 2am, so I didn't want to wake her. And I figured if I could temporarily slow the bleeding, I could drive Daisy to the hospital, which was only five minutes away.

I had raced inside and retrieved a scarf from my closet, taking it back out and tying it firmly above the cut.

When we reached the hospital, the staff at check-in immediately took her into one of the back rooms. I tried to follow but was advised to stay out the front to complete paperwork and keep out of the doctors' way.

Even though I worried Daisy wouldn't cope on her own, I had to trust that she was being cared for.

My brain is a blur of panic and randomness but all I can think of is how much blood my daughter has lost.

After what seems like forever, a doctor comes over. "Natasha?"

I jump up. "Yes?"

"We've got Daisy in surgery now, but she may need a transfusion. We're just waiting to see if everything stabilises."

An overwhelming sense of bleakness washes over me. A transfusion? "Um, she's type O negative, and I'm O positive, so is that going to be a problem? I don't think I can donate my blood to her."

"That's correct, but please don't be concerned. We have some here. I just wanted to let you know what was happening. But I also wanted to check, you put unknown on the paperwork for family history of haemophilia and other blood disorders?"

"Uh, that's right. As far as I know, there aren't any issues on my side of the family, but I'm not sure about Daisy's dad's side."

The doctor gives me a measured look. "Okay. Is there anyone you can ask? Like a paternal grandmother? Or aunt? We just don't want any unforeseen complications."

"Uh, I… I'm not sure."

"See what you can do, and tell one of the nurses if you find out anything."

I nod. The doctor leaves, and I think about how messed up this situation is. I have no idea about fifty per cent of Daisy's genetic history, and her dad doesn't even know she's in the hospital. All of Brad's family lived interstate, and he was estranged from most of them. As a result, he never made the effort to tell me any of their names or personal details.

But what if Brad *does* have some weird genetic condition that he's passed on to my daughter, and I don't find out until it's too late?

I have to admit, I've contemplated contacting my ex dozens of times over the past few years purely for administrative purposes, but I've never found a good enough reason to follow through.

I suppose today is it.

I never deleted the number I had for him, so I get out my phone and try it again. It goes straight to voicemail, and an elderly woman tells me to leave a message.

I suppose that means the number has been reallocated to someone else. I wonder if that poor woman gets irate phone calls from all the people annoyed at Brad. There used to be a lot.

I've made a point never to look for my ex on social media, but I realise that's probably the only way to reach him now. I open Facebook and type in his name. Brad Burns. Ugh. Even just thinking about the guy makes me ill.

And there he is, that arrogant face staring back at me. I wish I never had to look at him again but with my daughter being operated on and her health potentially at risk, I need to.

I click on the Message button and think about what I'm going to say to the man who abandoned us almost seven years ago.

> Hi Brad. I know you probably never expected to hear from me again, but I thought you should know that Daisy, your daughter, has been in an accident. She may require a blood transfusion. The doctors assure me she'll be fine but they've asked me to confirm any genetic conditions, including things like haemophilia, that run in your family. Can you please let me know ASAP?

I send it, not knowing what else to say.

I check my watch. I've already been here for an hour. I text Millicent to let her know what happened, and then I call Daisy's school to tell them she won't be in today.

I suddenly remember Lincoln. Our fight yesterday seems so frivolous now. I call his number, and he answers immediately, sounding as worried as me before he's even heard the news. It belatedly occurs to me that he may have thought I had left like Rachel, but I figure we'll talk properly once he knows what's happening.

I quickly explain the situation, and he jumps into action. I love that I can always rely on him to do the right thing.

He arrives in no time and races over to me, wrapping me in a hug. "Are you okay?" he asks, brushing my hair back from my face and gazing into my eyes.

"Physically, yes. Mentally, no." Tears start falling again.

"It's going to be okay," he says, making a heroic effort to sound confident.

"I'm not even the same blood type as Daisy," I wail.

"Do they not have any of her type stored here?"

"Yeah, they do. I just feel so helpless." I wipe the tears from my cheeks. "Actually, there's something I should tell you. I contacted Daisy's dad to let him know what was happening."

Lincoln's expression is wary. "And?"

"I haven't heard anything yet. I just wanted you to know since I never plan on keeping any secrets from you."

He pulls me back into an embrace. "I appreciate that, Tash, but you don't have to worry about my feelings now. Let's just focus on Daisy."

I'm about to tell him I want to resolve our argument from last night when Millicent charges into the waiting room. She quickly looks around, spots us, and runs over. "I came as soon as I got your text. Any news?"

I reluctantly pull away from Lincoln's chest and shake my head.

"Do you want me to go find a doctor? I can be very persistent when I need to be, and it's okay if they throw me out for being rowdy."

I manage to summon a tiny smile. "I'm sure that won't be necessary. They've been giving me updates when they're able to."

She looks at Lincoln. "Have you guys kissed and made up yet?"

Lincoln shakes his head. "Not officially. But I want Tash to know that what I said was stupid, and I would never ever want her to give up her dream. I'm in this for the long haul, and we're going to tackle every challenge that arises together."

I smile gratefully at Lincoln. "I'm sorry I overreacted. I know you didn't mean it that way. I was just being sensitive and worrying about history repeating."

As I say the word *repeating*, my phone beeps. I look down at the screen and see a message from Brad. I shakily scroll through what he's written and then look back at Lincoln, dazed. "Brad wants to meet up."

CHAPTER 36

LINCOLN

*U*gh. This is the worst. Of course Tash's ex would resurface at the most inconvenient time possible. Not only are Tash and I in a delicate place in our relationship but her daughter is in emergency surgery.

I suppress the urge to tell Tash to tell Brad to get lost and paste a supportive smile on my face. "What exactly did he say?"

"And what the hell is he contacting you now for?" Millicent demands.

"I had to ask him if there were any genetic issues we needed to know about on his side of the family. His message was actually quite caring."

Millicent looks at me and rolls her eyes. I nod grimly in agreement.

"Is he coming here?" I check.

"Oh, uh, actually, I'm not sure. That's probably not a good idea, huh? Although, if Daisy is in a bad way…"

Millicent wraps an arm around Tash's shoulder. "Honey, Daisy is going to be fine. Brad doesn't deserve to be here. He gave up that privilege a long time ago."

"Yeah, but what if he's changed?"

Millicent snorts. "Highly unlikely."

I ignore the queasy feeling in my stomach. I couldn't handle it if Tash's ex showed up and somehow convinced her that he was the better partner for their family.

Tash looks at me with realisation. "Oh God, Lincoln, please don't think me seeing Brad will have any effect on my feelings towards you."

"Hey, I fully support whatever is right for you." Although, inside, I feel my chest tightening. I hope this uneasiness isn't indicative of how our relationship is going to be moving forward.

"Okay, well since I do actually need to talk to him, I should probably agree to a quick meet-up. Will you both stay with me for moral support?"

"Whatever you need," I say.

Millicent shakes her head. "Fine. Although I don't know why he can't just answer your questions in a written message."

"Maybe he has a good reason for seeing me in person. I'll tell him we can talk for ten minutes."

"Anyone want a coffee?" I ask them.

"Uh, chai if they have it," Tash says, staring down at her phone screen.

"A large black coffee," Millicent says, giving me a sympathetic smile.

"I'll be right back."

I go in search of the hospital's café, my nerves threatening to overload despite my effort to stay calm.

I order two chais and a black coffee and wait for them to be made.

I think about how supportive Tash was of me when I first received the news of Rachel's betrayal, and I vow to be the same calming presence in return.

The scent of the chai takes me back to Channing's in Red Hill, and the way Tash selflessly looked after me that day. My heart swells with love, and I know I would do anything to make sure we get our happily ever after together.

I head back over to the waiting room and stop when I see another person with Millicent and Tash. So that's the infamous Brad.

Tash hasn't told me a lot about the guy, although from the way he ditched her, and from the stories her dad told me, I immediately dislike him.

His appearance doesn't do much to change my opinion either. His hair and face are perfectly groomed, and the ridiculously low scooped neck on his tight white T-shirt reveals an oiled hairless chest. Ick. I know I shouldn't compare, but how can Tash have dated someone like that and then be interested in me?

Millicent loudly clears her throat and looks pointedly in my direction. Tash hurries over and squeezes my arm. "Thanks so much for getting the drinks."

"No problem." I hand her one of the chais and carry the coffee over to Millicent. She practically snatches it out of my hand. "I definitely need this right now."

Tash awkwardly gestures at her ex. "Lincoln, this is Brad."

Brad doesn't seem to possess any sense of self-awareness and smiles widely. "Hey, dude. I watched you on *Sing To Me*. You were great."

"Uh, thank you?" I turn to Tash. "Any updates on Daisy?"

"No. But Brad has assured me there aren't any genetic issues we need to worry about, so I might go see if I can find a nurse to let them know."

She leaves me and Millicent alone with Brad, and I try to remember if I have ever been in a more socially awkward situation.

None come to mind.

"So you ditched my bestie seven years ago and decided to rock up now out of the blue?" Millicent says.

I hide a smile. Damn, I appreciate that woman today.

Brad holds up his hands in surrender. "Hey, Tash contacted *me*, and I felt like this was the right thing to do."

"You could have just told her what she needed to know via a written message and let that be it."

"Sure, I could have, but what kind of person would that make me?"

"Pretty consistent with your past behaviour."

I smirk. It's actually kind of fun being on the same side as Millicent when she turns all Mama Bear.

"Look, Millicent, I know you think you know what happened between me and Tash, but you don't. So don't go judging me when you haven't heard the full story."

"Actions speak louder than words, buddy. And I can see you've been missing in action for the last seven years."

He shakes his head in exasperation. "Same old Missy. I don't have to justify myself to you." He turns to me. "I didn't expect to see you here. Have you and Millicent been dating long?"

Millicent cuts in. "Uh, I hate to break it to you, sunshine, but Lincoln is *Tash's* partner. And if you had been paying attention, you'll see she's very much pregnant with his child."

An almost amusing array of emotions play across Brad's face. He looks at me with what I really hope isn't a competitive streak.

"I suppose congrats are in order then."

"Thank you."

"Now, this is what you're going to do when Tash gets back," Millicent starts. "You're going to tell her it was nice seeing her, and then you're going to go on your way."

Brad's face hardens. "Why do you always insist on meddling in other people's lives?"

"I wouldn't call being a friend meddling. Someone had to step up when you ran off like a freaking coward."

"I told you, you have no idea what you're talking about," Brad warns.

"Nothing you say can excuse your behaviour. At least Tash has a real man in her life now…"

I wave my hands in a calming motion. "Hey, hey. This kind of talk isn't doing anyone any good. It's a stressful enough morning as it is. Let's just all take a breath and focus on what's important. Right now, that's Daisy and Tash."

Brad plonks down on one of the seats far away from Millicent. "Fine."

I sit down beside Millicent at the other end of the room and gently place my hand on her shoulder. "It's not worth it," I say softly.

"Yeah, but he thinks he can just show up out of the blue with God knows what hidden motives," she hisses.

"We won't let him take advantage of Tash."

"No, we won't."

Tash returns looking a little less anxious. "I think everything's going to be fine."

I stand and wrap my arms around her again. "That's a relief."

"They're going to give her a small transfusion but it sounds like she'll make a speedy recovery."

"That's wonderful!"

Millicent inserts herself into the hug, squeezing tight. "I love you guys so much."

"We love you too, Missy," I say, laughing.

Tash steps back. "I should probably have a quick chat to Brad and then see him off."

"If you need us, just yell," I say.

"Will do."

I watch her summon Brad out into the hall and pray that he doesn't somehow find a way to charm his slimy ass back into Tash's life.

I don't trust that guy one bit.

CHAPTER 37

TASH

Seven years is a long time not to see someone. As I walk with Brad down the hall to the hospital's main exit, I sneak a side glance at the guy I once dated.

How did I ever find him a suitable partner? It's obvious he's a narcissistic douchebag just by looking at him. Who can spare that much time for grooming? And that oily chest? Gross. I swear he wasn't that bad when we were together. But maybe I was blinded by lust. It couldn't have been love. It was probably my pattern of going for guys who didn't show me much attention.

Even now, he's not acting as if he's glad to see me. I feel like some weird ornament tagging along beside him. Maybe I had nothing to compare to before, but when I think of my interactions with Lincoln, I know he's fully present, and we can communicate meaningfully.

"Are you still doing SEO?" I ask politely. That was the last career I remember him having.

He wrinkles his nose. "No way. That's a chump's game. Too much work for not enough return."

"Oh. So what do you do now?"

"I buy houses and flip them."

My eyes widen. "Really?"

"Yeah, it's a much more lucrative living."

"Probably high-risk though, huh?"

He frowns. "Not if you know what you're doing."

"I didn't mean to imply–"

"It's fine. You always did have a pessimistic personality."

I feel like I've been slapped. "Excuse me?"

"You never had any faith in the projects I wanted to do with you. You could be a multi-millionaire and living a life of luxury rather than slaving away on some kitschy business idea."

I don't know what to say. Clearly he's been following my career, otherwise he wouldn't have said that. But to be so insulting…

"Thanks for coming to see me when I asked, but I think I'm going to go back and check on Daisy now."

He shrugs. "Whatever."

I can't help myself. "Why *didn't* you just write me a message if there weren't any genetic issues in your family?"

"I thought you might have changed. Might have been interested in trusting me and letting me run our finances. We'd be a good team if you let me take the lead."

My brain feels like it's about to explode. "That makes no sense! You want to be a team but still be in charge? And what would I contribute, huh? The cash? And then sit back while you threw it all down the drain? Also, how does Daisy fit into this whole scenario? You haven't asked about her health once."

"Well, you did say she was fine before. I assumed you'd tell me if there was anything else."

"Oh my God! You're infuriating." I start walking away but stop at the last moment and look over my shoulder. "Don't worry. I won't make the mistake of contacting you again."

I don't hang around to wait for a response. The nerve of that guy! It sounded like the only reason he agreed to meet me is for capital for some questionable investment. I wouldn't be surprised if he hadn't even purchased his first house to flip. Brad was always all talk and no action.

I just hope he doesn't try to use Daisy as leverage to get what he wants in any future situation. At least he doesn't know where we live, and I can block him on social media. Lincoln's the only dad I want for Daisy from this moment on.

And I know he'd be honoured to take on the role.

Lincoln

DAISY COMES HOME the next day, and Tash invites me to stay at her house with them. I hadn't had a chance to give Tash my apology gifts, so I make sure I bring them along with me. Fortunately the roses haven't yet wilted.

After Daisy is safely tucked in for the evening, I sit Tash down and put the chocolates, flowers, and massage oil on the coffee table.

"I'm sorry again. I was an idiot. I know you have a history of not being treated equally in a relationship, and I should have realised that what I was suggesting could easily imply I didn't think your career had any value. But I promise that wasn't–"

She presses one of her fingers to my lips. "Shh, I know. I was being overly sensitive. You're nothing like Brad, and I shouldn't have put my insecurities or preconceived ideas onto you." She shivers. "God, that guy was a weirdo."

I smile, relieved. "Either way, I'll think twice before I speak in the future."

"You're kind of right about what you said though. As much as I don't want to admit it, I'm probably not going to be able to commit as much time to work as I want once the baby arrives. I'm going to start looking for an assistant next week."

"Once the tour is over, I'm going to take some time off so you can do whatever you need to. I've said before, I love all the craziness that goes with being a parent, and I want to be around as much as possible."

She throws her arms around me and holds me tightly. "I'm so, so lucky I found you."

"I feel the same. And I know I joked about buying a mansion, but I really would love for us to look for a new house together. I've got a potential buyer interested in my place, and I'm not sure your house would be big enough when the girls come to visit. Please don't feel pressured to make any decisions right away, but I was thinking if you didn't want to give this place up, you could rent it out… or put it on Airbnb…"

She pulls back and strokes my cheek. "Thank you for considering my feelings but I'm not tied to this place. I'd love for us to look for a new house together. I don't want you to bankroll the entire thing though. I want to pay half."

"I'm more than fine with that."

I suddenly realise that Tash's independent streak, while causing tension the other day, is actually a really good thing. I won't ever question whether she wants to be with me because of my bank account – and that's something that did occur to me more than once with Rachel – even before I went on *Sing to Me*.

"I guess it's lucky we live fairly close to each other, so we won't have to argue over which suburb to settle in," I tease. "But I also understand you wouldn't want to be too far from Daisy's school. Or Millicent."

Tash looks at the array of gifts on the coffee table and picks up the massage oil. "You're a sweet, sweet man. I think you deserve to benefit from some of these goodies."

I grin. "I won't argue with that. Should I take all my clothes off right now?"

She bursts out laughing. "I think we should both be wearing as little as possible." And then her face turns wistful.

"What?" I ask, smiling.

"I'm just thinking how crazy it is that I'm sitting here with you, and your baby is growing inside me." She reaches out and brushes her hands through my hair. "These curls... I dreamt about these curls for years, and now I can finally touch them anytime I want." She outlines the creases on the side of my mouth. "And these lips... I knew from watching you sing how amazing these lips would feel on mine..."

"You have an unfair advantage of knowing a little about me before I got to know you," I protest.

"I don't mind. We have all the time in the world to make up the difference." She leans in and buries her face in my neck. "And I couldn't know things like how amazing you smell, or how you really are as kind as you seemed on TV. I mean, I could guess, but it was so much better getting to learn that firsthand."

"I feel incredibly lucky that I was able to meet you when I did. I don't know what would have become of me otherwise. And while I can guess you started out as a fan, I really appreciated how you were there as a friend when I needed it most."

"I'm still a fan, Mr Page. In fact, I'm probably now your biggest one." She stands, pulling me to my feet with one hand and carrying the bottle of massage oil in the other. "Let me show you just how much."

I laugh. "Lead the way."

I follow her into the bedroom, knowing that even though life is not always going to run according to plan, I have this wonderful woman by my side.

CHAPTER 38

TASH

I'm not someone who enjoys being pregnant. And I'm also not someone who looks forward to giving birth (although, I don't know many people who do).

So when I feel the beginnings of labour starting, I am both glad that my pregnancy is coming to an end, but also filled with dread for the ordeal I'm about to endure.

It's 5am, so I gently tap Lincoln on the shoulder to rouse him. I still can't believe I'm having a baby with this man.

He rolls over, his mussed-up hair and adorable sleepy face making my heart melt.

"I think the baby's going to arrive today," I whisper.

That well and truly wakes him up. He immediately sits upright, eyes wide. "Really? You're in labour? Have your waters broken?"

I laugh. "No. I'm sure that's still a few hours away. The contractions are super faint. I remember with Daisy, they started about ten hours before she actually made an appearance."

"Yeah, but they say the second time is quicker. We should make sure everything's in place. Do you want me to call your parents?"

"Maybe let them sleep in a bit longer. We'll get them to pick up Daisy in a couple of hours."

He stares at me. "How can you be so relaxed about this whole thing?"

"Because I know we've got a long way to go."

"Can I get you something to eat or drink?"

"A cup of tea would be nice."

"Okay, you stay there. I'll be back in a moment."

"I don't need to stay in bed. In fact, I should probably walk around."

"Right, yes. Ignore me. Just do whatever feels right for you."

We decide not to wake Daisy up yet. Lincoln makes me the tea and then runs around the house like a madman, ensuring my hospital bag is packed and that the house is in order. I watch as he momentarily pauses at the door to the baby's bedroom. I go over to join him, looking in. It's all set up with a cot and blankets and a nursing chair. I can't believe there will be another person living here soon!

"I should tell Felix!" Lincoln says suddenly, getting out his phone.

"Yes, you do that." Felix is still in Sydney, but he's planning on spending some time in Brisbane in a few months. I teased him about being an on-call babysitter once he arrived, but he was surprisingly open to the idea. I think he might even be considering the possibility of having children himself someday. He's been dating a lovely guy called Ames for a while now, and although Felix assured me it was too early to really tell, he has high hopes for the relationship.

"Do you want me to text Millicent?" Lincoln asks.

"I've already done it. She's going to leave for the hospital at the same time as us."

I want both Lincoln and Millicent present at the birth. Mum and I don't have the kind of relationship that would suggest she'd enjoy being there, so she and Dad are going to look after Daisy and come visit once the action's over.

We're ready way too early, and we sit on the couch, looking at each other with a mixture of excitement and fear.

"This is it," I say. "There's no going back now."

"I would never go back." He strokes my hand reassuringly.

"Are you ready?"

"I guess we'll soon find out."

Lincoln

EVEN THOUGH IT was only a few years ago, I hardly remember the twins' birth. Rachel had to have a caesarean because one of the girls was breech, and it all got too complicated to attempt everything naturally. So all I remember was being given a gown and a cap and then watching a surgeon operate on Rachel's belly, intermittently shooting worried looks at Rachel's face. She handled it like she does everything – with very little emotion. In hindsight, I wonder if she was terrified I'd realise immediately that the girls weren't mine.

But I'm not going to think about that today. This little boy is definitely mine, and his mother is the love of my life.

We head to the hospital around lunchtime when Tash's contractions start making her double over. She tried to convince me we didn't need to hurry but I told her I'd feel a lot better if we hung out at the hospital instead, in case she's further along than she realises.

Millicent's waiting for us in the parking lot when we arrive, having already commandeered a wheelchair. She practically shoves Tash into it and wheels her inside.

It's lucky I insisted we leave home when we did, because within twenty minutes of arriving, the doctor confirms Tash is fully dilated, and the baby is on its way.

"Do you need any pain relief?" I ask.

"I think it's a bit late for that now," she huffs, shutting her eyes as another contraction hits.

"What can I do?" I feel so helpless watching the mother of my child in pain.

"Just be here." She squeezes my hand so tightly I feel it go a little numb. But that's a tiny price to pay if it helps at all.

I look over at Millicent, who's standing on the other side, also having her hand crushed. She smiles at me. I can imagine she'd much prefer that pain to what Tash is enduring.

After what seems like both no time and forever, the baby is out, and the doctor cuts the umbilical cord.

"Here's your little boy," she announces. "We'll just clean him up, and you can have him back."

I gently let go of Tash's hand and hover over the doctor as she weighs our child and wipes him clean. She expertly wraps him in a cute animal-print blanket and lays him on Tash's chest.

Millicent stays for a moment to snap a couple of photos but then claims she needs some coffee. I appreciate the chance for us to be alone for a few moments, and I stare at Tash and the baby in awe. "I guess we should figure out what we're going to call this little dude." We have a list, but we hadn't decided on a particular name yet, because Tash wanted to see what he looked like first.

She gazes down at his face. "I think he looks like an Oscar."

"Oscar Page," I muse. "I like it."

"What about a middle name? We should choose something a bit rockstar, don't you think?"

I grin. "Really?"

"Why not?"

"Because you know my favourite band of all time," I warn.

"I'm fine with that," she says, eyes twinkling.

"If you say so." I pick up my son and hold him close. "Welcome to the world, Oscar Zeppelin Page."

Life can throw you some crazy curveballs, but in my case, it's turned out better than I could have ever imagined.

I know from this point on, I can handle anything.

CHAPTER 39

TASH: THREE MONTHS LATER...

*M*y life is insane.

I don't know how I thought having a newborn, a business empire, and a partner on a world tour for several months would actually be manageable. I haven't slept for more than four hours straight since Oscar was born.

Lincoln had arranged to have four weeks off right after the birth, but then his contract required him to go back on the road. He's currently in Vietnam. I think. All the countries blur together after a while.

At least I ended up hiring an assistant, a lovely guy called Winston. He's been an absolute godsend, dealing with the dozens of emails I receive every day and basically filtering out all the little stuff I never realised took up so much time before. I think even when Oscar starts going to day care, I'm going to keep Winston employed full-time. My meals seem to have developed a bit of a cult following thanks to a feature on a national lifestyle show, and the supermarket chain is looking to expand my range next year. At that stage, we'll need a much bigger commercial kitchen, and I'll probably require multiple assistants.

Millicent has been a huge help, as has my mother, who took some time off work to come and help me with Oscar and Daisy.

Even Felix stayed true to his word and has been helping out a little since he temporarily located to a fancy rental in New Farm.

Daisy is in love with her little brother and still equally besotted with Lincoln. It makes me sad that she never got to know her real dad, but Lincoln treats her exactly the same way he treats Oscar. And once the tour is over, we'll all be able to spend more time together.

I've seen a few houses around town that I think Lincoln will approve of. Our aim is to have a new place by Christmas, because Isabella and Madison are coming over just after New Year, and we want to have a room for them to call their own.

I glance at the clock. It's 5pm on a Friday, and Millicent has insisted we reinstate our ritual of having a kid-free night once a month. My parents are due to arrive any minute and are going to look after Daisy and Oscar for three hours. That's as long as I can stand being away from them at the moment.

As if on cue, the doorbell rings.

Mum and Dad are standing there, with Millicent impatiently bouncing around behind them. They all look way more energetic than I feel.

"Where's my baby boy?" Mum asks, pushing her way inside and ignoring me in the process.

I point down the hall, while Dad wraps me up in a hug and kisses me on the forehead. "Hello, sweetheart. How are you feeling?"

"Tired. But I appreciate you babysitting tonight."

"It's no problem at all. Your mother's very excited to have an evening with her grandchildren."

Millicent steps forward. "We have to go, otherwise we'll be late."

"For what?" Millicent had given me the impression that we

were just going out for casual drinks and a bite to eat. I didn't know we were on a schedule.

"You'll see," she says mysteriously.

I look at Dad. "Do you know anything about this?"

"What do you mean?" he asks. My father has a terrible poker face.

"What are you all keeping from me?"

Millicent grabs my arm. "Nothing. Come on. Bye, Mr Northwood."

"Enjoy!"

"I'll be back for the 8pm feed," I promise.

He waves us off, and Millicent practically drags me to her car.

"What's the hurry?" I ask.

"Nothing. I just want to make the most of the time we have together."

I know she's lying, but I pretend to go along with her... for now. "Okay. So where are we going first?"

"I thought maybe we'd head over to Newstead for a drink."

"Newstead? Has a new pub opened up over there or something?"

"Yeah, I heard about this cool little place with personalised service."

"I'm intrigued."

We drive through the city, which isn't particularly relaxing since it's peak hour, but I'm still excited to be out of the house without a child glued to my chest.

It would be even more perfect if Lincoln was around, but I know his tour will be over soon. I just have to be patient.

We slow down out the front of The Triffid, and Millicent looks around as if confused.

"Are we lost?" I ask.

"No, I'm pretty sure it's around here somewhere. We'll park and walk the rest of the way."

"Whatever you think is best."

She points at a nearby alley. "Hey, I think I see an empty spot, but it looks narrow. Why don't you get out and wait here for a moment?"

"All right."

I climb out of the car and go stand near the entrance to The Triffid. It's all closed up today, but I smile as I remember the night I watched Lincoln play here. I still feel those same butterflies I experienced before we'd even kissed.

My phone beeps. Millicent has sent me a text. Weird.

> Go knock on the door.

I furrow my brow. Which door? The one to The Triffid? I look around, wondering what's going on. Where's Millicent gone?

I write back.

> Do you mean the door to The Triffid? Where are you?

> Millicent: Yes, The Triffid! I'll be there soon.

I look at the set of double doors behind me and hesitantly tap on one.

When nothing happens at first, I feel a bit silly. Is Millicent playing a prank?

But then suddenly one of the doors swings open, and a guy dressed in black is standing there.

"Come with me, please."

"Uh, who are you?" I ask, not moving.

"I'm from security. I have orders to bring you through."

"Bring me through to where?"

He points into the darkness. "Through there."

At this point, I start to feel more excited than nervous. Could this mean…?

I follow the man into the venue and make my way into the main hall. It's completely dark, and I stand in the doorway, waiting for my eyes to adjust.

The stage lights up, and someone is standing there, alone in front of a microphone with a guitar over their shoulder.

Lincoln.

I squeal and run to the edge of the stage. He sees me and his eyes light up, that swoon-worthy smile taking up half his face.

He doesn't say anything and instead positions his guitar ready to play.

He strums a chord and opens his mouth.

I was lost in the darkness
Nowhere to turn
Joy seemed so far away
But then you appeared
Like a star in the night
Leading me into the light
You are heaven sent.

I try to pay attention to all the lyrics, but I'm so overcome with happiness that tears start rolling down my face. How did I get so lucky to have this perfect man in my life? And how is he even here?

The song ends, and he puts the guitar down before reaching out and helping me onto the stage beside him.

"Hi," he whispers, tucking my hair behind my ear.

"Hi," I whisper back. "I thought you were overseas."

"I snuck back for a couple of days. It may mean I miss out on a little sleep, but that's a very small price to pay for the chance to see you again. And the kids. It was killing me being so far away for so long."

"I'm glad you're here but you didn't have to go to all this trouble for me."

"If not for you, then who?" he says, his gaze earnest.

"I love you so much."

"I love you too."

He steps back for a moment and gets something out of his pocket. "And to show you just how much I mean it, I want you to have this."

My eyes widen as I realise what he's holding. I stare at him and then back at the box. "Is this…?"

"Open it."

I shakily push the lid up, revealing a white gold band with a round-cut diamond in the middle.

He removes the ring from the box, holds my left hand, and gets down on one knee. "Natasha Northwood, we've gone through a lot in a short amount of time. And even though we've faced some pretty crazy challenges, I feel that it has only made us stronger. You are calm and kind and beautiful, and I would be honoured if you agreed to be my wife."

A lump in my throat threatens to prevent me from answering. I quickly swallow. "Yes. Oh my God. Yes!"

He laughs, stands, and gently slides the ring onto my finger. I hold it up to my face so I can admire this beautiful symbol of our commitment, and then I wrap my arms around his neck, pulling him close.

"Thank you," he says before pressing his lips to mine.

I breathe in his familiar scent and can't believe I'm connected to Lincoln Page in every way possible.

We'll be together forever, a beautiful and slightly unconventional family.

And it's perfect.

THE END

ACKNOWLEDGEMENTS

Thank you to everyone at Bloodhound Books. Betsy and Rachel, thank you for taking a chance on me! And Hannah, Tara, Morgen and Abbie – you have all been so lovely to deal with.

A huge thank you to Brooke and Lindsay for your helpful advice.

And of course, thank you to Diane. I'm very lucky to have you as an author buddy.

A special mention to Vikkie, also for being so supportive.

Lastly, an extra big thank you to Kesh, who is *my* own personal rockstar. :)

A NOTE FROM THE PUBLISHER

Thank you for reading this book. If you enjoyed it please do consider leaving a review on Amazon to help others find it too.

We hate typos. All of our books have been rigorously edited and proofread, but sometimes mistakes do slip through. If you have spotted a typo, please do let us know and we can get it amended within hours.

info@bloodhoundbooks.com

Printed in Great Britain
by Amazon

21505766R00140